The Gree..

Also by Christopher Bowden

The Blue Book
The Yellow Room
The Red House

The Green Door

Christopher Bowden

LANGTON & WOOD

Copyright © Christopher Bowden 2014
First published in 2014 by Langton & Wood
73 Alexandra Drive, London SE19 1AN
http://www.amolibros.com/bowden

Distributed by Gardners Books, 1 Whittle Drive, Eastbourne,
East Sussex, BN23 6QH
Tel: +44(0)1323 521555 | Fax: +44(0)1323 521666

The right of Christopher Bowden to be identified as the author of
the work has been asserted herein in accordance with the Copyright,
Designs and Patents Act 1988.

All rights reserved. This book is sold subject to the condition that it shall
not, by way of trade or otherwise, be lent, resold, hired out or otherwise
circulated without the publisher's prior consent in any form of binding
or cover other than that in which it is published and without a similar
condition including this condition being imposed on the subsequent
purchaser.

All the characters in this book are fictitious and any resemblance to
actual people, living or dead, is purely imaginary.

British Library Cataloguing in Publication Data
A catalogue record for this book is available from the British Library.

ISBN 978-0-9555067-3-4

Typeset by Amolibros, Milverton, Somerset
www.amolibros.co.uk
This book production has been managed by Amolibros
Printed and bound by T J International Ltd, Padstow, Cornwall, UK

One

The church clock was striking ten. A strident reminder of the lateness of the hour, mournful and insistent, as if chiding her for being there at all. The door clunked to a close. She stood for a moment on the worn top step of Number One Partridge Court, flanked by a pair of standard bay trees in square lead planters. The midsummer sun was well below the surrounding roofs now but the court itself, enclosed on three sides, retained the heat of a sweltering day. Clare Mallory was struck by the sense of calm and quiet, reinforced rather than disturbed by the steady splash of the fountain in the middle and the distant buzz of traffic on the Embankment.

Number One housed the chambers of Gordon Russell QC, a barrister of flair, energy and brilliance admired and feared by his opponents. Rated 'a first class set' by *Wise Counsel* magazine, the chambers comprised some forty barristers practising in a wide variety of fields. Clare was one of them, called to the Bar six years earlier and considered 'a promising junior' by the same magazine. Plaudits from anonymous but well-satisfied clients declared that she was 'sensible, level-headed and shrewd', combining 'an intellectual grasp with a pragmatic approach'. Quite why she failed to demonstrate these qualities outside the office during the events of the following weeks was something on which she, and others, would have cause to reflect for some time to come.

She made her way over the cobbles, past the familiar cluster of red brick buildings. Solid and reassuring, they exuded a sense of continuity and tradition, discretion and quiet confidence. The benches outside them, normally packed at lunchtime, were deserted at this hour. Even she was rarely here this late, preferring to stay on to tackle a last-minute brief than cart the bundles home.

Without warning, a figure stepped into the sickly glow of a lantern sprouting from a bracket on the wall.

"Ill met by moonlight, proud Titania."

It was James Daly, twenty-six going on forty-five, dripping sweat in the Harris tweed suit and bright yellow waistcoat in which it was rumoured he had been born. He was only a little less handsome than Mr Toad, the nickname bestowed by the clerks of Boswell Buildings where he had at last secured a tenancy.

"James," she said, her heart pounding. "Don't do that."

"Sorry, my dear. Did I give fright?" It was hard to believe he was younger than Clare.

"How are you, anyway? I hear that congratulations are in order."

"Indeed, indeed. I'm uncommonly fine, thank you, and not a little dandy. What a splendid evening."

With that, he straightened his bow tie and shuffled away, past the last remaining Ferrari in the car park to the discreeter bike racks down the ramp on the other side.

A narrow escape. Had he been waiting for her, lurking in the shadows beyond the lantern's reach? The thought was unsettling. Thank goodness he didn't linger longer or suggest a visit to the wine bar. After half a bottle of the house claret, James had revealed ('vouchsafed', as he might have put it) at a previous visit to Benchers that his interest in Clare was more than professional. Only the timely intervention of her friend Jessica had enabled a tactful departure and undue loss of face.

She went through the archway at the bottom of Middle Temple Lane and strode to the Embankment, pausing briefly to look across the river to the buildings on the South Bank and the final, snatched reflections of a dwindling sun. As she headed towards Temple underground station, she was suddenly overwhelmed by tiredness; the hours of concentrated work without a break were taking a toll. She needed to be at home. She raised a tentative arm; a taxi screeched to a halt. From force of habit, she gave the driver the address of her Hornsey flat, only to remember some minutes later that she had recently moved. Luckily, he was in high spirits and had no objection to turning round and going south of the river.

Two

Number twelve Mulberry Grove was a two-storey, flat-fronted house in a run of properties that looked much the same when seen from the street, apart from a spot of post-war infill near The Golden Goose, a local pub that attracted customers from further afield at Sunday lunchtimes when jazz was played upstairs. At the rear, the houses had been altered and extended in various ways. Not least number twelve, whose previous owners, Roland and Marcia Turnbull, had built an uncompromisingly modern kitchen extension, predominantly glazed, designed to complement what remained of its early Victorian host. The architects had described it as a 'box of light', providing a desirable increase in floorspace to meet the needs of a twenty-first century lifestyle; the neighbours had called it an eyesore that was out of keeping and damaging to residential amenity. Ten years on, no one remembered what the fuss was about or even noticed it was there.

The Turnbulls had commissioned furniture for their new extension, including an oak table of such enormous dimensions that it would not fit into the Wiltshire cottage to which they were about to move. They agreed with Clare to leave the table and its eight matching chairs for a modest consideration plus her own more manageable scrubbed pine affair and an odd assortment of kitchen chairs.

It was on this large oak table that Clare placed a small card shortly after the taxi had delivered her safely to the gate of number twelve. Not the card the driver had given her in lieu of a proper receipt but the one she had found on the mat next to the bill that represented that day's post. She lined it up with the others. Five of them now, each a different colour but all saying the same thing in gilt letters: 'MADAME PAVONIA. Clairvoyant. Your future told, your problems solved.' No contact details, no other information to suggest how anyone could avail themselves of Madame Pavonia's services. Even if they wanted to.

The latest one was blue, following on from red, orange, yellow and green. Five days, five cards, five colours. A rainbow sequence, thought Clare, but incomplete. Were there two more to come? Then what? They were well produced but why go to the trouble and expense of printing them and pushing them through letter boxes without revealing where Madame Pavonia was based or how to get in touch with her? Perhaps, she reflected, it was the start of a wider campaign or was softening people up for personal visits.

Anyway, what problems did she want solved? She didn't have time for problems. Not her own at any rate, what with Jessica's shameless affair with a married man who never quite got round to leaving his wife and her feckless brother's inability or unwillingness to secure gainful employment after the trouble he had caused the family last year. On the other hand, Jessica and Duncan had been an item for a while now and seemed pretty relaxed about it. And at least Colin got work from time to time with that Enigma Theatre Company, not that you could call acting a proper job with prospects.

She hauled herself up and over to the freezer to find something microwaveable, did what was required and slumped back at the table with a glass of wine to wait for the beeps.

Indigo and violet slipped through the door on succeeding days, as expected. Rather satisfying, she felt, to predict what a fortune-teller was going to do, even if the pattern was fairly obvious. Yet why the cards were sent was no clearer. Quite the contrary; brief mention of the rainbow series in snatched conversation with the neighbours on either side met with blank looks and shaken heads. Just the usual collection of junk mail, they said: instantly binned, the only cards among them advertising plumbers, tree surgeons, mini cabs and the like.

It was not a comprehensive survey, of course. Other occupiers of the terrace may well have had Madame Pavonia's material. But somehow she thought not. Whether it was her or the house that was being targeted was another matter. Few people had her current address. The cards could have been meant for Roland and Marcia. She had spotted a few books of the mind, body, spirit sort on the shelves when she first came to see the house. Not a very Roland thing, surely. Maybe Marcia had contacts in the psychic world, in which case the cards could be some kind of private joke among members of the fraternity or sorority or whatever they were called.

Clare pressed her forehead against the glazed door and stared into the garden, landscaped for the Turnbulls by a celebrity gardener when the extension was built and now well matured, despite replacement of some of the less resilient specimens that had succumbed to frost. A small stand of silver birch at the end shimmered in the late morning sun; tall grasses swayed in a gentle breeze. In the glass of the folding door, a reflection: seven rectangles of colour, end to end, along the edge of a large table.

The sharp metallic click of the letter box. On the hall carpet, floated beyond the mat, a plain white sheet of paper. She picked it up and turned it over. A Grand Summer Fair, she read, taking place the following Saturday. It was in the local park, once the grounds of a Palladian mansion when this area was still in the country and The Golden Goose was an isolated building called The Mulberry Inn. After many years languishing under Council control, the mansion had been refurbished and now accommodated a smartish restaurant with a function room on the floor above.

A Great Day Out! Fun for all the family! The flyer proclaimed a startling array of attractions in a startling variety of fonts. Dog-walking and gymnastic displays she could do without, falconry and sheep-shearing had left her cold at the 'country fête' held in the grounds of Gordon Russell's Suffolk home last year, and fire engines from the local station held little allure. Even if the men were in uniform. The community and craft stalls might be worth a look, she thought, and so might the horticultural club marquee. And at the bottom of the sheet, squashed in like an after-thought, the simple statement that a fortune-teller (Madame Pavonia) would be present at this year's fair.

The door of number twelve had begun to blister in the scorching sun. The chrome knob, one of the Turnbulls' anachronistic additions, was painful to the touch. Clare held it with a handkerchief as she pulled the door to and set off towards the park, feeling slightly furtive in dark glasses and Italian straw hat. Focussed on the matter in hand, she did not notice the battered white van on the other side of the street. It started up and followed her progress, heedless of the traffic building up behind.

She heard the fair well before she saw it. Over the Tannoy, ear-splitting announcements about lost children, the avoidance of litter, and the day's unmissable events were punctuated by blasts of 'Summer Holiday' and other songs thought appropriate to the season. A pound coin tossed into an empty ice cream tub on a table at the park gates bought her a lucky programme and entrance to the fair.

It was too hot to push and shove in the hope of bargains. She maintained a sedate pace as she moved along stalls that sheltered from the sun in stuffy gazebos, looking as best she could over heads and between shoulders, darting forward when gaps appeared. A few new hardbacks at a fraction of the published price – review copies, the woman said; some hand-made cards; two jars of apple chutney; a pottery badger for Jessica. Basket bulging, she made her way to a stall selling iced lemonade, oblivious of the man in the sweat-stained tee-shirt loitering nearby with a glass of beer in one hand and a mobile phone in the other.

She saw the tent beyond Professor Swozzle's Punch and Judy show, the booth silent until the next performance later in the afternoon. The professor himself, aka children's entertainer Ron Gently from Tooting Bec, was taking advantage behind the booth with a slice of frittata on a paper plate. The tent, she thought, would not have looked out of place at the Battle of Agincourt. With broad stripes in yellow and red, it was round and had a pointed roof. A sign propped against a barrel said:

MADAME PAVONIA
Famous Clairvoyant
Your future revealed, your questions answered
Special offer for Summer Fairgoers
Today only
£10 for a half-hour session

The canvas at the entrance of the tent parted abruptly as a red-haired woman, pale as milk, left in haste, snaked between stalls and was absorbed by the crowds beyond. Clare walked past, turned by the Rotary Club tombola, and ambled back again. She was in two minds. This was her chance to put a face to the name on the cards, she told herself, to find out why they had been put through *her* door and no one else's. On the other hand, she could be wrong about being singled out and what on earth would she say then? Either way, there seemed little prospect of sustaining a conversation lasting anything like the allotted thirty minutes. She pretended to look at postcards on the local history society stall while she decided what to do.

A man with a mobile phone was stationed outside the tent, as if to prevent other potential clients from entering. He had the seedy and menacing air of a night-club bouncer. But as she approached he looked up, spoke into his phone and slid away.

She took a deep breath, pushed through the thick gauze inner curtain and penetrated the body of the tent. It was hard to see in the gloom after the brightness of the sunshine she had left behind. Her foot caught the edge of a rug laid over the grass. She stumbled forward and steadied herself on the back of a chair.

"Care, my dear." She started at the sudden intervention. A voice from nowhere, rather mannered, almost theatrical, to Clare's ear but with more than a trace of Cockney in the mix.

As her eyes adjusted, she made out a woman at a round table covered in a green cloth, the crushed velvet lustrous in the light of a candle burning low. The woman waved her to sit down. Clare saw not the veiled Gypsy fortune-teller she had imagined, all rings and bangles and topped by a turban, but a neat woman in, what, her mid-ish sixties?, conventionally dressed for a summer's day, set apart only by the thick woollen shawl round her shoulders. She was staring at a small sphere, balanced on a wooden stand in the middle of the table. The ball glowed in the soft light of the candle.

After the warmth outside, the air of the tent felt cold. Clare rubbed the goose bumps on her bare arms, struck by the intensity of the silence. It was becoming oppressive. She shifted in her seat, basket clamped between her feet, straw hat balancing uneasily on top. When would something happen? Was she supposed to speak first?

"Madame Pavonia…?"

"Indeed," she acknowledged, with a gentle incline of the head.

"Not tarot, then, or palmistry or…tea leaves," said Clare, for something to say. Her courage had deserted her. She felt foolish and tongue-tied, not at all the brisk and confident young barrister from Partridge Court. "You use a glass ball."

"A *crystal* ball is my chosen tool. I stay true to it. This is natural quartz, my dear. Do not underestimate its power."

"No. Sorry," she said, fingering the gold locket that dangled at her throat. "I just…"

"How may I help you? Have you suffered a loss or bereavement? Do you wish to make contact with a departed? Or do you seek guidance in matters of love or the direction of your life?"

"Er, nothing specific. Just curious, really. I saw your cards and your name on a flyer."

"Ah, yes. Let us see what counsel we may give you. But first I fear we must attend to the money side. I find it best to deal with this before a reading; it is so easy to forget by the time we have finished."

Disposing discreetly of the ten pound note, Madame Pavonia asked Clare to put her hands on the table, close to the crystal but taking care not to touch it. The fortune-teller shut her eyes and appeared to relax, breathing slowly and evenly. Her lips moved but no sound emerged. Was she in a trance? Gradually, she unclosed her eyes and gazed into the ball. Clare noticed it had minor cracks and imperfections. They caught the light of the candle and sparkled.

"I see the number one. Perhaps you are alone or too self-reliant. I see a well. It runs deep. You keep your feelings hidden or reserved for someone or something important. I see a ship or a boat. It is capsizing. This could mean a failure to communicate with a person in the past."

Madame Pavonia looked more deeply into the ball and frowned.

"I see a tower: you feel trapped or imprisoned in some way, maybe in a job or a way of life. There is a bridge. It offers an opportunity, but use it wisely. Once that path is taken, there is no going back. Yet there is a barrier, a wall, an obstacle that must be overcome before progress can be made. Or perhaps it is some resistance on your part. I see the letter P...and a hand outstretched. This could be someone you know who wants to help you. Even if you do not yet realise it. Even if you do not think you need such help.

"Does any of this make sense to you, my dear, provide some pointers that may assist you in life's journey? If you have any questions, do feel free to ask me."

Clare stared for a while into the flame of the candle, guttering, sputtering its last. Madame Pavonia leaned back in her chair on the other side of the table and coughed gently. Then Clare said, "Thanks but it's rather all-purpose, isn't it? A bit indefinite. I mean, it could apply to pretty well anyone. To a greater or lesser extent. And are we talking past, present or future?"

"Life is a continuum. The future becomes the past soon enough. The present is barely the blink of an eye."

"The board outside says you reveal people's futures."

"I *see* their futures, as a rule. Sometimes it's best not to reveal all that I see. People are looking for a positive outcome."

"And in my case?"

"The crystal remained cloudy. Whatever was there was obscured." Madame Pavonia faltered. "There is nothing I can add."

"What do you mean?"

"My dear, I saw no future."

"I have no future?"

"The crystal offered nothing that I could interpret with any certainty beyond the symbols I mentioned. It happens sometimes."

"Where does that leave me?"

"My advice would be to reflect on what I said earlier. Do you know who P might be?"

Three

She said I had no future."

Clare took another sip of rosé and put the glass down with a chink on the metal table. They were sitting outside on Jessica's new Yorkstone patio, bathed in the soft apricot light of a summer's evening. Jessica had crossed the river a couple of years earlier than Clare, leaving her small east London flat for a Georgian house in Camberwell that was much too big for her. "At the moment," as she put it. It was her one extravagance, the rest of the fortune she had inherited having been invested. For the time being, she continued to work at city solicitors, Quarrenden and Cox.

"She claimed she could see nothing at all. Nothing beyond some nonsense about bridges and towers, which mean whatever you want them to mean. So much for being a 'Famous Clairvoyant'."

"Don't worry about it," said Duncan, taking a generous swig. His wife, Clare had learned from Jessica in the kitchen, was on her way to a residential training course in Cumbria. Allegedly. "She's obviously a crank.

One person's future, so-called, doesn't depend on whether somebody else can see it or predict it. Anyway, she was clearly wrong as you're here now. Alive and kicking, as far as I can tell."

"Now isn't the future."

"It was when she said you didn't have one. Or rather, it was the present still to come. Strictly speaking, the future doesn't exist."

"How do you make that out?"

"Well, how can it?" said Duncan. "It's just a label, a convenient term to cover everything that hasn't yet happened. And if things haven't happened, they can't exist, can they? The future is just the present in abeyance. A potential present, if you like."

"But the present lasts no time at all. Barely the blink of an eye, as the fortune-teller put it. As soon as it happens, it's over. It's in the past. It's a continuous process, like a conveyor belt of infinite length; the passage of time, in fact."

"I suppose you could say the present is just a transitional phase between two periods of non-existence."

"So the past doesn't exist either?" said Clare, reaching for the bottle.

"Of course not. It's just a dustbin for all the presents that have been and gone, ceased to exist, crammed full of ex-nows. Only the present is real. Everything else is either before or after."

"It's nonsense to say the past isn't real. It must be if it's happened. The fact that the moment's over doesn't change that."

"It doesn't exist."

"It doesn't need to exist to be real. It's enough that it existed once. What's real is the fact that it happened."

"You're confusing time and events," said Duncan. "The fact that it happened isn't the thing itself."

"But you can't have time without events, can you? Time doesn't exist in its own right, only in relation to what happens."

"Hm. I'll give you that one. But I'm not sure about the 'passage of time', though. Things happen in the order or sequence they do but that's not the same as time passing or flowing, even if that's how it's perceived. I'll get another bottle."

"Is that what people mean by 'time's arrow'?" said Jessica, stepping through the French windows with a bowl of olives in one hand and something cheesy in the other. She put them on the table and retrieved her glass. "Sorry. I got stuck on the phone with my mother."

"This is worse than a day in court," said Clare, spearing an olive with unnecessary force.

"I've never understood which way the arrow is supposed to go, have you?"

"Well, it must be forwards, not back."

"From the past to the future?"

"I suppose so. You can't have effect before cause."

"Or is it the other way round? Things are future before they're past, aren't they?"

"According to Duncan, neither exists."

"Quite," said Duncan, bending to top up their glasses.

"And, as I was saying, there's no such thing as the flow or passage of time."

"Well, Madame Pavonia says that life is a continuum."

"Who is Madame Pavonia?"

"The fortune-teller we've been talking about."

"What sort of name is 'Pavonia'?" said Jessica. "It sounds like a fictitious country. Out of Gilbert and Sullivan or the Marx Brothers or something."

"Could be the Lord Leighton painting," said Duncan. "That's called 'Pavonia'. You know, the one they used on the poster for that exhibition at the V and A a few years ago. A sultry beauty, raven-haired."

"I don't think Madame P quite fits the bill."

"Or explain why the picture's called 'Pavonia'."

"Probably from 'pavonian'," said Duncan. "Pertaining to the peacock. There's a fan of peacock feathers in the painting, as I recall. Peacocks were a symbol of the aesthetic movement."

"What's this got to do with Clare's fortune-teller?"

"I've no idea."

"I may have missed something," said Duncan, through a mouthful of seafood salad. They had adjourned to the kitchen, the dining room being home to Jessica's exercise bicycle and rowing machine. Her new badger had joined the others on the dresser. "But why did you go to this person in the first place?"

"It was the cards through the door. I told Jess. Every day a different colour but all with Madame Pavonia's name on them. I don't know why they came to me.

No one else seemed to get them. Then, when this fair came along and I saw she was at it, I thought I'd go and have a look."

"Did it explain why you were singled out? If you were, that is."

"No. I meant to ask but somehow I didn't and then it was too late. But at least I saw who she was and what she was offering. I paid ten pounds for the privilege. She gets people to pay up-front."

"She obviously has it down to a fine art."

"I don't begrudge that so much. It's the locket I'm concerned about. I've had it since I was twelve."

"Not the lovely one your grandmother gave you? I wondered why you weren't wearing it," said Jessica.

"I know I had the locket when I went into the tent this morning. I just can't remember if I came out with it. My mind was on what Madame Pavonia had been saying. As soon as I realised, I tipped everything out of my bags in case it had fallen in and then went straight back to the fair. But the tent had already gone. There was no sign of her or the locket. Just a patch of trampled grass and a few holes where the stakes had been."

"How on earth could she dismantle a tent and take it away so quickly?" said Duncan.

"I suppose she must have had help."

"She can't have taken the locket, surely?" said Jessica.

"I don't know," said Clare. She sounded despondent.

"Did you ask if it had been handed in?"

"Yes. It hadn't. Hardly surprising. Who'd hand over a

Victorian gold locket, if they found it? Not to mention the chain."

"Most people, I'd have thought. But what about Madame Pavonia herself?" said Duncan. "Do you know where she lives?"

"The organisers were a bit difficult at first, started going on about confidentiality and data protection. They were already cross she'd left early. So I put on my best barrister voice and said I would have no option but to involve the police and wouldn't be surprised if the press got to hear about it. Did they want the publicity? That did the trick."

Four

The house was at the bottom of a quiet road, lined with horse chestnut on one side and high walls and hedges on the other. A small oasis of rural calm, the man with the dog had said when Clare asked for directions, having, as it turned out, walked past the end of the road several times without spotting its name. The signs had been removed only a few days before by a person or persons unknown more interested in their value as scrap than the convenience of people trying to locate the entrance to The Nook.

The building was set well back behind large wooden gates so that only its chimneys and slate roof were visible from outside. The gates were tight between a pair of brick pillars, topped by stone. On one of the pillars she glimpsed a sign, a faded rectangle partly obscured by ivy. She held back the shiny leaves to reveal the name of the property: The Coach House. It had once served a grander residence, according to the man with the dog, but the evidence had long since disappeared, thanks to a direct hit by the Luftwaffe and final demolition of what little remained in the early 1950s. Now the grounds were occupied by Mansion Drive, a cul-de-sac of detached bungalows, with a discreet entrance off the main road.

As she looked round for a bell or knocker or some other means of attracting attention, she noticed that one of the double gates contained a small door. It was slightly ajar. A gentle push and she stepped into a cobbled courtyard with raised beds at the edges, held in place by rows of sleepers. Her foot caught an errant fig, startling a robin that flew from the handle of a watering can to a place of greater safety in the wisteria that clothed one wall. On the other side, lilac clematis twisted through climbing roses, crimson and pink and white. The scent of sweet peas on willow wigwams filled the air. A sleek black cat, curled in a bird bath, was oblivious of Clare and of the insistent murmur of bees seduced by the lavender nearby.

"She's right. You *have* put on weight."

Clare wheeled round in fright. A woman tottered from the shadow holding a glass. Lengths of hennaed hair, free from the restraint of clips and combs, tumbled about her shoulders. Her baggy trousers and linen shirt, both a faded aquamarine, were heavily creased, as if she had been sleeping in them. The woman steadied herself against one of the cast-iron columns supporting the glazed roof that projected from the house.

"I thought at first you were that dreadful Mrs Manticore from over the road. Blocks the road with her recycling sacks and never flattens her boxes." She raised her glass between finger and thumb and shook it. "Drink?"

Clare declined and said, "I was looking for Madame Pavonia."

"Iris isn't here. Came back from that fair yesterday all atwitter. Couldn't settle but wouldn't say what it was. If you ask me, she hasn't thought this through."

"Iris is Madame Pavonia?"

"Of course," said the woman, swaying gently. "The one and only Iris Peacock. Former member of the Peacock Sisters, 'the celebrated Sydenham Chanteuses'. She was the eldest." Clare looked blank. "A bit before your time, perhaps. She reinvented herself as a psychic when the sisters went their separate ways."

"When will she be back?"

"I couldn't say. She packed her bag first thing, shoved in a couple of crystals and drove off in Juno. That's her car."

"Not big enough for a tent, I imagine."

"She's not gone camping."

"I mean the tent she used at the fair. How did she move it?"

"The boys see to that side of things. It doesn't come here."

"I didn't catch your name," said Clare.

"Marigold. Marigold French. Resident artist and general dogsbody. I share the house with Iris."

"What did you mean I'd put on weight?" She felt herself bridle and tried to control it. "Or was that your Mrs Manticore? We've never met, have we?"

Marigold turned with some care and beckoned Clare to follow.

"I'll see if I can find it."

She installed Clare in a wicker chair in her studio and disappeared into the body of the house. No north-facing windows and cool, clear light in this room. The one-time conservatory was filled with sun and much else. Every available surface, Clare saw, was covered in bottles and jars, brushes and tubes of paint. A large jug of roses, obviously cut from the courtyard a day or two before, dripped petals on to the tiled floor. In one corner, a folding screen partly obscured a deep ceramic sink that may once have been white. And at the far end, a cork board, pinned with postcards and pictures snipped from magazines: still lifes by Cézanne, another by Morandi, fruity faces from Archimboldo, trees along a stream that could have been Corot. Below the board, stacks of canvases, faces to the wall.

Clare got up and went over to the easel set roughly in the middle of the studio. The only canvas in the room exposed to view was held firmly in place. Three fish lying side-by-side on a plate. It was large and oval and powder-blue. A couple of lemons nestled in one corner of the picture. She looked closely at the fish, admiring the markings, the iridescence, the silvery sheen. What *were* they? Mackerel? Herring? Rainbow trout? The work looked unfinished but of their subject there was no sign.

"You can thank Peevish for that," said Marigold,

bending at the doorway to stroke the cat that had abandoned the warmth of the bird bath. She appeared a little steadier on her feet. "The day before yesterday. I only left the room for a moment to answer the phone. The next thing I knew the beast had run off with a fish and was devouring it under the table. Not before he'd mauled the other two."

"Do you only paint still life?"

"I do these days. So much easier than people. At least a bunch of grapes keeps still, doesn't get cramp and doesn't complain or answer back."

Marigold led Clare through a dingy corridor to the sitting room beyond. A comfortable room with yellow-ochre walls and a pale grey marble fireplace. Against one wall, as if standing to attention, a longcase clock with a lunar dial: a furtive moon, frozen in flight from a pack of marauding stars. Above the mantelpiece, a small picture with a country scene and, to its right, a tall vase with peacock feathers. Clare felt the eyes staring at her, alert, accusing, unblinking. She looked away.

A sheet of paper lay on the coffee table. Marigold picked it up and said, "I found it on Iris's chest of drawers. It's some time since I saw it last but I never forget a face."

Clare recognised it straightaway, even upside down. She reddened and felt slightly sick.

"How did she get this?"

She took the sheet from Marigold, almost snatched it, and sank to the well-padded arm of the settee. It was a page from the website of Number One Partridge Court. The page about her, listing her qualifications, the areas of law in which she specialised, and the highlights of her relatively brief career. She looked at the black-and-white photograph at the top. She *had* put on weight since it was taken: too little exercise and too many visits to Benchers' wine bar. It was clear from the date at the bottom that the page had been printed several months ago.

"Got it off the internet, as you can see. She came across your name in connection with one of your cases. Can't think which one it was off-hand."

Clare made a mental note to check the details of the cases she had done at the beginning of the year. "Why should she want to know about me?"

Marigold shrugged but said nothing.

"So she must have known who I was before I went into her tent. The whole thing was a charade."

"Are you sure you won't have a drink?"

Clare slid to the settee itself and looked at the sheet again. In the photograph, taken only a few years earlier, a slimmer, younger self. The short, dark hair, at least, much as it was now. She was wearing the locket. How could she have forgotten why she was here?

"Did Madame Pavonia…Iris…have my locket when she came back from the fair?" She gripped the glass of chilled white wine and took another sip.

"She did say something about a locket. But not that she had it or that it was yours."

"*What* about it? What did she say?"

"Nothing I could follow. She was in a bit of a state."

"Is it here?"

"I've not seen it."

"It could be in her room."

"Not that I noticed when I was looking for the page about you," said Marigold. "I can't turn the place upside down."

"Do you know where she's gone?"

"To the cottage, I imagine. That's where she usually goes."

"Didn't she say?"

"She left in rather a hurry. Probably assumed I'd know."

"Can we…I…get hold of her by phone?"

"The cottage doesn't have one. That's one reason she likes to go there. Gives her space to think without being interrupted. It's like a retreat."

"Mobile, then."

"That would defeat the object. Her object, that is. She left it in the pin tray on her chest of drawers. She'll be back when she's ready. She always is. I'm afraid you'll have to be patient."

Clare put the empty glass on the table and sat in silence, her head resting on the back of the settee. Ahead of her, over the mantelpiece, hung the picture in its plain wood frame. She looked at it more closely this time, taking care to avoid the peacock stare. A watercolour of a small house in a landscape, nestling in a hollow, isolated and exposed but for the stand of trees nearby, a house of mellow brick and grey-white stone with a green front door. In the bottom right-hand corner of the picture, two red initials – NP – and a date she could not read.

Five

*I*ris pulled sharply into the lay-by and screeched to a halt.

"Sorry, Juno," she said, righting her tapestry bag in the passenger seat and removing a bottle of water. "My mind's wandering. You know what I'm like when I'm in a pother. I need to collect myself." At the far end of the lay-by, a large refrigerated lorry lumbered to the exit, giving her and Juno the area to themselves.

She took a swig, and then another, and returned the bottle to the bag beside her. She pushed her seat back a notch or two and sat, hands in lap, half-watching a jackdaw on the verge, separated from the swish of traffic on the Brockley road by the thickening hawthorn hedge.

After a while her breathing became more even. This is unravelling, she thought. I should never have agreed to do it. Just a favour, they said. For old times' sake. A fright; nothing more. No real harm. Nothing in comparison, anyway.

She started to hum. A distant, melancholy hum,

scarcely the vibrant rendition of 'Chattanooga Choo Choo' that had had them shouting, screaming for more that last night, the very final public performance of the Sydenham Chanteuses. Shimmering, swaying, pink and gold. What was the name of the place? The pub with the stage the other side of Peckham Rye? Had a stuffed parrot in the Ladies. Ivy something, or was that the woman behind the bar?

Must have been a good thirty years ago now, she thought. Iris, Evie and Joan: the Peacock Sisters. Evie and Joan were Peacocks no more, of course. One marrying a south London builder, the other something in the printing trade, both rapidly producing broods that still refused to leave the nest. Layabouts, the lot of them. More trouble than they were worth, especially whatsisname, Joan's eldest. Gary, that was it. Gary Parslow. Hardly a name she should have forgotten.

She saw the sisters from time to time. It was always much the same: reminiscing about the old days, repeating stories that might have been funny once, talking of comebacks ("How about changing our name to The Hot Flushes?" said Evie), comebacks that would never happen. She sighed and fumbled for a mint.

She should have resisted when they mentioned the fair. But they made it easy: paid the stallholders' fee, hired the tent, put it up – and taken it down again, sharpish. And the truth was it had been a while since she had done any fortune-telling at all – in public, at any rate. Just the odd psychic fair, like the one at Blackheath where she had first met Marigold. A lot of the old gang were switching to the internet or giving readings over the phone. Mystic Mavis; Hermione Lux; Stanley Scrimshaw; even Gypsy Jones, the Orpington Oracle: all had gone that way – but there was no substitute for human contact, such as it was.

They had given her a brief and that piece about the girl they had printed off a few months earlier, round about the time it happened. So she had had some idea of what to expect and how to play it. Even so, it was clear straightaway that Clare Mallory was no push-over. There was an odd tension within her, though. Much more than was usual. Fiercely resistant, defiant, yet wanting, needing, to get something out of the process, even if she didn't know what it was. And the reading itself was perfectly genuine, as far as it went; it was a pity the girl didn't seem to take it seriously. A great pity.

What she hadn't bargained for was the locket. It was lying on the rug with the chain curled round. It must have come off when the girl had grabbed her hat and basket and marched off with barely a word. As soon as she picked the thing up she had felt it and once she had prised it open there was no doubt at all.

Six

*P*uddles on the platform and droplets on the seats. It had rained during the night. But a blear of sun in the milky sky above the sycamores on the other side held promise of another warm day. Familiar faces in familiar places. No pushing or shoving as passengers took their turn and boarded the seven twenty-two.

Clare slipped into her usual seat in the second carriage from the front and surveyed the scene. Not too full yet. A man eating a banana, another doing the crossword, a sharp-fingered girl dipping into a small make-up bag extracted from the larger bag beside her.

She had a conference later in the morning at Partridge Court with solicitors from Quarrenden and Cox. Jessica's firm, not that their paths had crossed professionally. They went back further, to St Luke's; a brief overlap (her last year, Jessica's first), meeting again at one of those college reunions that seemed to come round with increasing frequency.

She was not concentrating on the case. She had slept badly as the events of the last forty-eight hours went round and round in her mind. The tent, the locket, the encounter with Marigold. The session with Madame Pavonia was obviously a set-up, the so-called reading a sham. OK, so she lived alone. What of it? Lots of people did. And what was wrong with being self-reliant? It was a strength, not a weakness. As for the nonsense about having no future, each passing hour showed that for what it was, whatever Duncan may say about the future not existing anyway.

She touched the place where the locket should be. The small gold crucifix she had found in her jewellery box seemed light and insubstantial but she needed something to fill the gap. She had to get the locket back but it wasn't certain that Madame Pavonia, Iris, actually had it and even less clear why she would have taken it in any case. Perhaps, she thought, she should have pressed Marigold for the address of the cottage and asked Jessica to drive her there.

At least she could look up the cases she had been involved in around the time that sheet from the chambers' website had been printed off. They might offer some clue about what was going on, at any rate until she could confront Iris Peacock when she was back from her cottage.

The train slid into another station. Ingress of rucksacks, Polish plumbers with tool bags, a woman in purple who squashed in next to her and jiffled to a tune heavy with throbbing bass notes.

Clare clutched her briefcase, held it close on her lap. The book inside remained unread, as it had these past few days. She stared, unseeing, at the back of the seat in front. She had had that locket for the best part of twenty years, she reflected. Given to her by her grandmother upstairs in the Somerset house while her brother Colin and assorted cousins rampaged in the garden and parents enjoyed a few child-free moments out of sight. Sitting on the bed, smoothing the silky eiderdown, while her grandmother removed a wad of discoloured tissue paper from the chest of drawers and brought it to her. Clare unwrapped it slowly to reveal the locket and its fine gold chain. It was oval, engraved with a fern leaf, snug in the palm of her hand.

"It was given to me when I was twelve too. By my great-aunt Sarah. A long time ago now. You can open it if you want."

Her grandmother had to do it for her, prising the locket apart with firm thumbs to reveal two compartments: in the front, a sepia photograph of a girl with long pale hair about her shoulders; in the back, a curl of the hair itself; both held firmly under glass.

Clare still had the tissue paper, largely disintegrated in a shoe box along with other childish things, but now the locket she had worn every day since coming to London was gone. Its loss felt like a betrayal, a betrayal of her grandmother and of memories of the time they spent together.

She started as she felt a hand on her arm.

"Are you all right?" asked the woman in purple. "We're at Victoria."

"Sorry, yes, I was miles away."

*

It was early evening before she had the place to herself. She had forgotten Gordon Russell's drinks to welcome the newest member of chambers, Romilly Meek. Formidably bright – Cambridge Double First, Harvard Law School, fluent in French and German, prizes galore. There she was, the centre of a semi-circle by the fireplace, the audience of largely middle-aged men hanging on her every word. Perched on a window seat on the other side of the room, Clare felt woefully inadequate as she sipped a modest manzanilla, half-listening to Jeremy Wicken-Fenn outlining his plans to purchase a share in a vineyard in the Loire. Perhaps, she thought, she should go on a diet, join a gym. If only she had the time.

Declining the invitation to adjourn to Benchers, she stole back to her desk and looked up her schedule for the month before that page was printed from the chambers' website. Not much help. A week at home with the parents in Oxbourne – she still called it home – followed by another visiting her brother when he was back in Paris with the Enigma Theatre Company. Why did everyone else seem to go to Madagascar or Sumatra or walk the Inca Trail to Machu Picchu?

The fortnight before was peppered with personal injury cases: workplace incidents, a few slips, trips and falls, a couple of road traffic accidents. All with a twist of one sort or another that had inhibited settlement of claims before they got anywhere near the courts – and with pretty successful outcomes for the claimants she had represented. But there was nothing about the cases or the people involved that stood out, despite some gruesome details of the sort she used to find distressing. She had become inured to things like that.

She turned to the previous month. The odd seminar, articles for the chambers' newsletter, some hearings in Nottingham and Lincoln. A reference to Grayson v Parslow. Yes, a messy case. It was coming back to her. A hearing before District Judge Meldrum in that brutalist building in south London the County Court shared with the Crown Court. Whiplash injury to neck and back after Parslow's van smashed into her car as she waited in a queue at traffic lights. The outcome was compensation to her client, Sonia Grayson, of some £6000.

She recalled her first glimpse of Parslow – tense, pale, angular – on the other side of the crowded waiting area as the minutes passed before the case was called. Sonia, still fragile, wary nearly two years after the accident, looking away so as to avoid his eye. In the courtroom, a bad start for the defence as Parslow refused to swear and had to be persuaded to affirm instead. And giving evidence, he was nervous, tentative, unconvincing.

He denied liability: it was just an accident: no one could reasonably have foreseen it or be held responsible for it. The van had an unsuspected defect that prevented him from stopping in time. Alternatively, even if there had been any negligence on his part, that did not result in the claimant's injuries or the damage to her car. These were a consequence of her braking suddenly and without warning well before the end of the queue for the lights.

His barrister struggled on his behalf in the face of contrary witness statements and the van's own maintenance records. District Judge Meldrum was not impressed and chided the parties for not reaching settlement sooner. His decision was not in doubt.

Be that as it may, there was no connection she could see with the page about her that Marigold had retrieved from Madame Pavonia's chest of drawers. Or with the performance in the tent at the weekend. Nothing to suggest why she should have been singled out. Perhaps she had given Parslow a bit of a hard time that day but not much more than defendants in other cases. OK, so he lost but his insurers would have picked up the bill.

Seven

*I*ris parked Juno in the usual place by the wood pile, retrieved her bag and headed for the front door. It had been a while since she was here but nothing by way of letters, leaflets or newspapers impeded the opening of the door as she huffed through with her bag. The cottage was off the beaten track and hardly anyone had her address.

From the top of the bag she removed the bread, milk and other items she had bought in Brockley village some miles back and took them into the lean-to kitchen at the rear of the cottage. It felt cold and damp despite the heat of the day. As she waited for the kettle to boil, she peered through the grubby windows, past the froth of elder in flower by the boundary, over the hedge and across the emerald fields descending gently to the floor of the valley below. The frantic boiling of the kettle clicked sharply to a halt and rapidly subsided. Now there was no sound, no sound at all, but for a thrush's tapping of snail on path and the distant caw of unseen rooks.

Her father, Nathan, had bought the cottage for a song donkey's years ago. They used to come here in the Morris Oxford, walk on the downs, trespass in the grounds of Brockley House in the days the Brockley family still owned the place. Parents died, sisters married, the cottage came to her. No one else was interested. Visits with men friends when it suited, the lean time after her husband Arnold became a departed, occasional weekends with Marigold before she gave up painting *en plein air* and confined herself to still life in the studio. It had been Nathan's studio once. A talented amateur water-colourist, he exhibited many times at the Summer Exhibition. She still had some of his paintings.

She knew she couldn't put it off any longer. It had to be confronted. She drew the curtains to shut out the light and brought a candle to the table she had dragged in front of the empty fireplace. As the candle sputtered into life, she carefully rolled a crystal sphere from a velvet bag and set it on the wooden stand in front of her. From a second bag she plucked a scrap of bubble wrap from which she removed the locket.

She had sensed it the moment she found the locket on the rug in the tent, picked it up, brought it to the cloth. The vibrations were unmistakeable. They spelled a troubled history: a life, a death, many years before it passed to Clare Mallory. And when she had opened the locket – that photograph, that hair – she felt spirits long dormant had been disturbed.

She placed a hand on the sphere and closed her

eyes. The energy was weak, the forces unsettled. The vision was cloudy but the cloud was thinning. It was a mourning locket; the curl of hair cut from a child shortly after she had died. And the photograph had been taken only shortly before. Towards the end of the nineteenth century, she guessed. A girl of ten, eleven, frozen in time. She was ill, not expected to live long, but that was not how she died. The event was sudden, unforeseen.

I see a tree: a family connection or some link with ancestors? Or perhaps related to the death itself. It has leaves but is losing them. An autumn occurrence or maybe signifying a brief life coming to an end. And an axe: yes, symbol of a life cut short but could it be the instrument of her demise?

Iris shivered. The cold was bitter, clinging. The candle was low and beginning to smoke.

I see the letter B…Bea…Beatrice. The girl's name. And the colour red: anger, aggression, a hint of flame.

She opened her eyes and gently prised the locket apart. She looked at the photograph, drawn to the space to the right of the girl's head. There was something there. It was the face of a man, faint but unmistakeable. A man with a penetrating stare. She cried out and the face was gone. Was it a clue to the past or a warning for the future?

How much, she wondered, did Clare Mallory know of the locket's history or of the girl captured inside it? There was a line from Beatrice to Clare. Not direct, of course, but direct enough. They were certainly related. Of that Iris was sure.

She thinks of the locket as a talisman but there is danger here.

Eight

*T*he warm light of the setting sun, filtered by trees at the end of the garden, played gently on the wall behind Clare's head. She did not notice. She was sitting at the kitchen table with two buff folders in front of her. One brought from the filing cabinet in the study upstairs, the other pulled roughly from the briefcase now slumped against a table leg on the floor beside her.

The first was labelled 'CONTENTS INSURANCE'. She opened it and leafed through documents relating largely to her Hornsey flat until she found the clutch of valuations. Not the ormolu clock now residing on the mantelpiece in the sitting room she hardly used, nor the figures she had bought in a Paris flea market that had turned out to be Chelsea, nor the diamond and sapphire ring she had inherited from her other grandmother. She halted at the sheet about the locket. A concise description: Victorian mourning locket: fine condition: engraved with fern frond to front, plain to rear: opens with period photograph of unknown girl on LH side, lock of hair presumed to be of girl on RH side: hinge in good order: nine carat gold: hallmarked Birmingham 1886. Then a bit about the chain.

The monetary valuation had been disappointing – barely enough these days for dinner for two in a decent restaurant – but that was not the value to her. She looked at the photographs clipped to the sheet; some showing the locket life size from various angles, others with it blown up to enormous proportions. She had never looked at them carefully before. There had been no need: she had always had the real thing close to her.

She had to get it back. She was certain that Madame Pavonia had found the locket somewhere in the tent, had it with her in her country cottage. What she could not understand was why the clairvoyant should have taken it there and what she intended to do with it.

Clare paused. An over-large photograph of the girl, startlingly detailed if a little fuzzy at this scale. Long fair hair, centre parting, falling loosely around the shoulders. Not obviously brushed, it looked unkempt, almost wild. No hair band, clips or ribbons to keep control. And the girl's eyes, dark-circled, staring straight at the camera yet dull, vacant, apparently unseeing: no hint of the suppressed giggles she remembered from childhood snaps. Posed in a studio, by the look of it, with no domestic artefacts or garden features to distract. Just a single flower held in a raised hand against the pleated front of a plain white dress.

Hardly a lively portrait, she thought, but not a lifeless one. Not like those awful cases she had come across where photographs of Victorian children were taken after they had died. Yet this girl must have died young – it was a mourning locket, after all – and perhaps not long after the picture had been taken. Around the mid-1880s, presumably, but what was her name, what had happened to her? Clare could not remember if her grandmother had told her all those years ago. With the locket's loss, she felt a pressing need to know more about the girl lost with it, trapped inside, here but not here, reaching out to her in some way. It was the least she could do.

She closed the folder, slid it to one side and poured another glass from the bottle that had surely been full only a moment ago. She drew the second folder towards her. It contained a single sheet, a copy of the original on the loose-leaf file held securely in the office at Number One Partridge Court. It was the report of the case of Grayson v Parslow she had contributed to the legal yearbook's monthly digest a little while ago.

Back and neck: whiplash injury: no previous condition

G, female, aged 53 at the date of the accident and 55 at the date of the hearing, suffered injuries as a result of a road traffic accident when her vehicle was struck from behind.

P's van was driven into the rear of her car as she remained stationary in a queue of traffic in the approach to lights at a junction. G's vehicle was shunted into the car in front as a result of the collision. G sustained a whiplash injury to the neck and lower back strain.

G required seven weeks off work. She attended hospital on the day of the accident and visited her GP on a number of subsequent occasions. Physiotherapy treatment began five months after the accident and, following treatment, there was a substantial improvement in symptoms. She continued to have low-grade symptoms, arising mainly from the back, at the date of a medical examination some 18 months after the accident and still suffered similar symptoms at the time of the hearing.

G experienced flashbacks for the first few weeks after the accident. She felt anxious for several months when travelling by road, whether driving or as a passenger, constantly checking the rear-view mirror. The anxiety had largely resolved at the time of the hearing.

General damages £6250.

Nine

*I*ris moved her chair to a patch of shade and adjusted the cushion. Grouped about her, hostas in pots, none the worse for her neglect, were coming into flower, some mauve, some lilac, some white. From the stand of beech nearby came the rasp and chatter of chasing squirrels, around trunks and over branches, ignored by pigeons strategically placed to catch the remaining sun. High in the sky, the glint of a plane. She imagined passengers looking down at her looking up, an insignificant dot in a wooded landscape.

She should never have kept the locket. She knew that. And she knew where Clare lived; the boys had told her. The girl must be missing it; the locket clearly meant a lot to her. She could easily have put it in an envelope and slipped it through the letter box after dark. But the vibrations had been too strong to resist; she needed to know more. She had not worked out what to do, how to deal with the nagging unease that the locket held a threat in some way she did not yet understand, that Clare herself might be at risk.

What if the girl had been to the house, met Marigold, asked questions? Come to think of it, that was not unlikely given what she had gleaned of her character that day. There was no knowing what Marigold might have said. She was unreliable at the best of times and highly unpredictable after a glass or two. Surely, she would not have mentioned the cottage or given the girl the address. Probably not, as there had been no sign of her or anyone else.

She subsided and bent to retrieve a mug of herbal tea, sipping absent-mindedly for a while. Then she sat back and closed her eyes, still nursing the mug between two hands.

She recalled her first meeting with Marigold at the psychic fair in Blackheath. Marigold sidling up to her small table inserted at the last minute between Mystic Mavis and the fire exit. She was in a right two and eight: wan, bruised, hunched over the bag she was clutching so tightly it seemed she would crush it. Iris had gone through the motions but it was clear that what Marigold needed was refuge from a man who made her drinking look a model of sobriety.

Iris had decided there and then to take her in. Impulsive, some had said, but the arrangement suited her too. It was good to have another human presence in the house after the lonely years since Arnold had shuffled off his mortals. Marigold provided companionship of a more useful sort than Peevish, doing a bit of cooking and gardening when the mood took her. And it pleased Iris to see her father's studio – for years a dumping ground for things she preferred to forget – being put to good use again. Iris herself reverted to her maiden name of Peacock and psychic Iris Gorringe became Madame Pavonia, famous clairvoyant.

She drained her mug and sighed. If only Marigold would sell more of her paintings, have an open studio, take pupils, do something to make things easier. She must have another word with her at the right moment.

It had been her brother-in-law's idea, the cards. "A different colour for every day of the week." Printed them himself after-hours in the works by the railway. The boys had taken it in turns to deliver them to the house in Mulberry Grove, the address discovered by having Clare followed back from chambers one night. "Serve her right," they said, but it was Madame Pavonia's name on the cards, not theirs. And on the flyer too.

Ten

Clare decided to walk from the station to the house in Mafeking Avenue, staying close to buildings and boundaries to take advantage of the shade before the heightening sun eliminated it for several hours to come. She felt guilty that it had been so long since she had been back in Oxbourne. A cancelled case conference and last minute out-of-court settlement gave her an unexpected day to see her parents – and do a little research.

Her route took her past the public library, a High Victorian extravaganza where she had spent so many Saturday mornings in her time at St George's. The school was still there on the other side of the by-pass but the library that had served the town for over a hundred years was, she learned from the posters outside, under threat of closure. She needed no persuasion to swish through the sliding doors and sign the petition inside. She gave her address as number twenty-six Mafeking Avenue, the house at which she arrived, pink and panting, some fifteen minutes later.

*

She had been uncertain how to broach the subject. In the event, her mother saved her the trouble through the simple expedient of asking where the locket was. Clare touched her throat and said, "Oh, at the jeweller's. The hinge looked a bit wonky so I took it in. The crucifix is just filling the space for the time being. It felt funny without something there."

After lunch, Clare said, "The jeweller asked who the girl was, the girl in the locket. I didn't know; I don't remember Grandma saying, though I suppose she must have done when she gave it to me."

"Her name was Beatrice," said Janet Mallory. "She was the younger sister of Grandma's Great-aunt Sarah, the one who gave the locket to her. And their brother Augustus was Grandma's own grandfather."

"Hang on. So, he's my great-great-grandfather. Which makes Beatrice my great-…great-…great-aunt. I'm related to her." She felt the loss of the locket more keenly. She dabbed her eyes with the sleeve of her blouse. "Sorry. It's just… She was only…It's a mourning locket, isn't it? How did she die?"

"I've no idea. Scarlet fever, perhaps. Or consumption. One of those Victorian diseases."

"What a waste. Does she have a grave somewhere?"

"I imagine so. But I don't know where. Does it matter after all this time?"

"I just wondered. She seems more real now I know her name and that she was an ancestor of mine."

"Of us both. There might be something in the box."

"What box?"

"The one with all Grandma's papers and photographs and things. Where's your father?"

Eric Mallory struggled in to the sitting room with a large black box. He lowered it to the floor with a thud as the greasy rope handles slipped from his hands.

"It looks like a seaman's chest," said Clare, reaching for the box before her father was even upright. She lifted the lid with ease. It was hinged along one side and kept upright by chains at either end. The box was crammed with files and folders, envelopes and packets and bags, neatly arranged but with no clue as to their contents.

She looked up and said, "What time's the last train?"

Eleven

*N*either Clare nor Jessica favoured Benchers. Too many people they knew and a better-than-evens chance of another unwelcome encounter with James Daly. They settled on Tasso, the wine bar in the City where Jessica had once brought Duncan. She said he was back home in north London, checking proofs of the second volume of his series on animals in art. Clare bit her tongue; the perennial question of whether he would ever get round to leaving his wife again went unasked. Anyway, it only invited discussion of her own position, on which she had had to endure a gentle grilling in Oxbourne. The stock reply that she was simply 'between boyfriends' was beginning to wear a bit thin.

"Duncan was right about Madame Pavonia and peacocks," said Clare, planting two glasses of chilled white wine on the marble top of a table that looked like the base of a sewing machine. "Her name really is Peacock. Iris Peacock, one-time member of 'the celebrated Sydenham Chanteuses', apparently. So celebrated that I'd never heard of them."

"You've tracked her down? But where's the locket?"

"I went round to the house but she had already fled to her rural retreat, leaving her friend Marigold in charge. Somewhat the worse for wear, if you ask me." She decided not to mention the page from the chambers' website; it would only raise questions she could not answer. "Marigold didn't know when she'd be back and said there was no way of contacting her in the meantime."

"But does she have your locket?"

"Marigold was a bit coy about that. She says it's not in the house. I think Madame Pavonia took it with her for some reason."

"That's ridiculous. What about the police?"

"I don't want to go down that road if I can help it and I can't prove she has the locket in any case. I rang the house last night – I picked up one of Marigold's cards in her studio – but there was no answer. I'll give it one more try and then I'm going to the cottage myself."

"Where is it?"

"I don't know; I'll have to get it out of Marigold."

Jessica stayed silent as she sipped the remains of her wine then volunteered to get two more glasses.

"It would have been cheaper to buy a bottle," she said brightly.

"Her name's Beatrice," said Clare. "The girl in the photograph – the one in the locket. Turns out she was my great-great-great-aunt."

"Turns out? I thought you'd had the locket for twenty years."

"Best part of. Well, if I was told when Grandma gave it to me, it didn't register or I'd just forgotten. Children don't take much interest in family history, do they?"

"How do you know now, then?"

"My mother. I popped down to Oxbourne. She told me – and produced a great box of Grandma's papers I didn't even know we had. I was looking through them for hours."

"Anything of interest?"

"Lots. I took pages of notes and pictures of some of the photographs. Look."

She dipped into her bag and produced her phone.

"This is Grandma as a girl in the early 1930s; in the ATS during the war; on her wedding day; then holding my mother as a baby; and there she is with me, as I remember her."

"Nice. Funny to see the locket on someone else, isn't it?"

"Where?"

"She's wearing the locket in the first picture, though not in any of the others."

Clare scrolled back through them.

"You're right; she must have put it away for safe-keeping."

"Who's the man, by the way?"

"What man?"

"In the first one; the one with the locket."

"There's no man; just Grandma. See."

"Sorry. I thought I saw a face. Just there," said Jessica, pointing to the space to the right of the girl's head. "It must have been a reflection."

Clare sat at the kitchen table with the old St George's exercise book she had used to take notes. Scattered around it were papers and photographs she had liberated from the Oxbourne box when it became clear she was running out of time.

Beatrice's surname was Newton, the maiden name of Clare's grandmother too. Well, it would be, she thought, the brother, Augustus, being Grandma's father's father. Born in 1876, Beatrice died only eleven years later in 1887, the year after the locket was hallmarked. Did they commission it before she died or just buy it from a shop that had had it for a while? There had been no death certificate among the papers to confirm whether Beatrice had died of scarlet fever, consumption, or something else entirely.

The whole of her short life was spent at Danby Hall, a house in or near the Norfolk village of Great Danby. The family, it seemed, left the house shortly after her death and did not return. Clare picked up a sepia photograph, reproduced as a postcard, showing the outside of the Hall. Relatively modest, she thought, by country house standards: stucco and gothic windows, finials and crenelations, set behind the yew hedge that separated it from a large area of grass and a group of trees that could have been elms. Another postcard showed the drawing room, heavily panelled, crammed with furniture, ornaments and plants in pots. But no people in either picture or in any of the other views that shared the packet in which she had found them.

She turned to the scrapbook she had come across at the bottom of the box. Its cover was dull, faded. She made out the words in neat black copperplate: 'Miss Beatrice Anne Newton, March 6th 1885.' Inside, pages of shiny cut-outs, neatly stuck in. Fruit and flowers, butterflies and birds, plump cherubs and bad-tempered kittens. Cautionary tales of boys and girls who failed to heed parental advice, quotations from Shakespeare and minor poets, all transcribed in the same orderly hand.

She leafed through to a series of sketches: rabbits, hedgehogs, doves and what she took to be various parts of the garden at Danby Hall. Fairly repetitive but surprisingly competent, she thought. And then some caricatures, whether drawn from life or works of imagination she could not tell. They started innocuously enough ('a cheery fellow', 'a helpful soul', 'a good sort'). Abruptly, the gently mocking style took a darker turn: twisted faces and haunted eyes, unkempt hair and jagged teeth, grasping hands and claw-like fingers. The captions had vanished; just a few words scrawled at the bottom of the page in a frantic script little resembling the ordered copperplate that preceded it: 'When shall I find peace?'

Clare shuddered and reached for the cardigan on the back of her chair; the air in the kitchen had grown chill.

She was in two minds about whether to carry on,

shaken less by the images themselves than by the fact that they had been produced at all. It seemed scarcely credible that this was the work of a girl of eleven, or however old she was at the time. Somehow, it seemed likely that Beatrice had drawn them towards the end of her life – and the remaining pages in the scrapbook were entirely blank.

It was a while before she resumed, fortified by a glass of rosé, a handful of cashews, and the comparative warmth of the garden. She sat outside, head back, eyes closed, lulled by the splash and splatter of the water feature next door, before dragging herself back to the table. Her spirits were not lifted by the rectangle of mourning card, embossed with weeping angels and edged in black, that she did not remember retrieving from the box at Mafeking Avenue.

In Loving Memory
Of
BEATRICE NEWTON
Who died June 10th 1887
AGED 11 YEARS
Interred at St Peter's Church, Great Danby,
June 23rd

A couple of weeks before she was buried – and in summer.

A light is out
A voice is stilled
A place is empty
Which can ne'er be filled

She read the verse again through tear-filled eyes, and then once more. Pull yourself together; you come across worse things every day at work.

As she stood up to find something she could stomach in fridge or freezer, she noticed a photograph fallen to the floor. She held it between thumb and forefinger under one of the kitchen spotlights. It was a picture of three small children crammed into a cart, copious trellising and big windows ranged behind. In front of the cart, secured to its shafts, a blinkered goat was waiting patiently for the ride to begin. She flipped the photograph over and strained to read what was pencilled on the back. She made out three letters: A, S and B. Augustus, Sarah, and Beatrice.

Names, faces, places. The more she learned, the more she wanted to know. She felt herself being drawn in; it gave her life a spark of interest largely lacking outside the world of Partridge Court. She had nothing special planned for the weekend and Norfolk wasn't far.

Twelve

Clare put a pound coin in the wooden box that was fixed to the wall and paused to admire the arrangement of flowers – pale pink peonies and dark red roses – that greeted those entering the church by way of the south porch. As she looked about her, other arrangements of varying size and complexity loomed at strategic points in the body of the building. The ladies of the parish had been busy. She took in whitewashed walls and gothic tracery, pitch pine pews and cheerful kneelers, bright stained glass and burnished brass. A comfortable church, she thought, but it would not do to linger. Her business lay outside and it could take some time.

In the churchyard, she opened the guide to St Peter's she had just bought. It was a thin document, printed with no great skill on shiny paper and decorated with sketches and photographs in black and white. It had been written half a century ago by a previous incumbent, the Reverend Francis Japes MA, and revised at irregular intervals in the years since. St Peter's, she learned, was one of a group of neighbouring parishes that included St Mary's Nestling and St Giles' Addleshaw. Burials no longer took place in the churchyard at Great Danby but at the larger one in Nestling, though cremation, she read, remained the preferred option.

She looked across to the rows of headstones, pallid and pockmarked, set like giant teeth in new-mown grass. Unused the churchyard may be but at least it is neatly kept. She wondered how to find where Beatrice was buried. The guide said that many of the late Victorian graves were concentrated towards the eastern end 'but that is by no means an invariable rule'. The optimism she had felt when the taxi dropped her by the lych gate was beginning to wane. Why had she thought the task would be straightforward? She left the gravel and took the grass path that led towards the yews at the far wall. The crenelated tower of flint and clunch was behind her as she moved roughly parallel to the long low nave and chancel.

She worked methodically among the stones, weathered and worn and scarred by lichen. Names and dates were barely legible. A cluster from the 1880s raised her hopes but yielded nothing. She steadied herself against the memorial to one Emily Brandon that rose beside her and gulped water from the bottle she pulled from her bag. Where to go next? She was tempted to ask the man she had seen from the corner of her eye standing by the rain barrel at the end of the church whether there was a map or plan or some other record of people buried here. He looked as though he tended the place, judging by his clothes and the sickle in his hand. Yet when she turned round he was no longer there. The churchyard was deserted.

She had to get out of the sun. The yews offered shade and she made towards them. It was pleasantly cool under the trees. But as she approached the wrought-iron bench on which she had intended to sit for a while the air became chill, deathly cold. Nettles and long grass lay scattered on the ground, hacked rather than cut and recently by the look of them. They had not even begun to wilt. Then she saw it: protruding from the severed stalks, a small grave, better preserved than most.

Clare knelt, rubbing the goose bumps on her arms, and read,

> BEATRICE NEWTON
> 1876 – 1887
> She fell asleep too soon.

Beneath the words, the image of a dove, carved into the stone.

She tidied the grave as best she could, wrapping a handkerchief round her hand to avoid being stung, and took some pictures on her phone. A resentful toad left the scene and loped towards a patch of dock.

The woman with the dog-collar and a large bunch of keys introduced herself as the rector, the Reverend Jenny Virgo. She jangled closer and peered at the map that Clare had printed off the night before.

"Are you lost?"

"Just trying to get my bearings. I'm heading for Danby Hall. Looks like I want Church Road, then Cock Lane."

"If you're walking, it would be quicker to take the footpath; it brings you out by the entrance." The rector pointed to the sign roughly opposite the lych gate.

"Thanks. Nice church. Welcoming…well kept. Does the man with the sickle look after the churchyard by himself?"

The rector looked puzzled. "We mow and strim at St Peter's. I'll pass your kind words to the churchwarden, Valentine Ogg. You may see him at Danby Hall, of course." With that, she went into the church and closed the door.

The church clock was striking two as Clare reached the beginning of a driveway. A discreet signboard in burgundy and gold confirmed that this was the entrance of

DANBY HALL
HOTEL AND RESTAURANT
Conference facilities available.

The building itself was hidden from the road by trees, mostly pine. But as she made her way along the low grass bank that bordered the drive she caught the glint of sun on windscreen, heard the chink of glasses, the clatter of cutlery. She hoped they were still serving, having had nothing to eat since the snatched croissant at Liverpool Street station at a time she would normally be in bed on a Saturday morning.

She knew that Danby Hall had long ceased to be a private house. It had been a school for some years, the website said, requisitioned during the war for purposes that were not entirely clear, later the management training facility of a well-known bank, and subsequently a hotel briefly trading under the name of 'The Pines' before reverting to its proper name. How far the building and its gothic interiors had survived these changes of use remained to be seen – the soft focus boutique images on the website were not much help – but she had brought the pictures from her grandmother's box, just in case.

And then it came into sight. Not the sepia view of Danby Hall lodged in her mind but fresh cream stucco, crisp and clean against the clear blue sky. Rather smart, by the look of it. She felt underdressed, had qualms about entering, until a couple in jeans and tee-shirts came out of the front door and headed towards the car park.

Her plan was to have a quick look round the place, or as much of it as was open to public gaze, and then order a taxi back to the station in Marsham. Things began well enough. Salmon and broccoli quiche, green salad, and a glass of the house white set her up for a stroll round the grounds. There was no sign of the trees in the photograph, the ones she had thought were elms. The thick yew hedge that once separated the house from the main lawn had been removed at some point and replaced with hornbeam. The glazed extension at the back of the building accommodated a swimming pool, to judge by the muffled splash and squeal that came from it. The glass was too misted to see in. The big windows on either side looked like the ones that featured in the picture of the Newton siblings and the goat cart.

She sank to a garden seat of vaguely Chinese design and pulled an envelope from her bag. She was only yards from where the photograph must have been taken. She felt a rush of excitement – to be here, to be so close. Augustus, the eldest, playing the man in charge with affected hauteur; the girls wedged in beside him. Sarah with a confident smile for the camera, Beatrice apprehensive, even frightened, gripping her sister's arm with one hand and the side of the cart with the other. She almost seemed to be looking at Clare, appealing to her.

The restaurant was empty now as Clare cut through, the tables cleared of debris and set for dinner. It was an elegant room in contemporary style and clearly not the original dining room of the house. Past the unmanned reception desk in the entrance hall – portraits, mirrors, flowers, displays of brochures of local attractions – and on to the residents' lounge. She pushed the heavy mahogany door and went in. She recognised the old drawing room, panelling still intact, but it felt stark stripped of the late Victorian clutter of the photograph.

The room was cool and quiet, any residents having better things to do on a fine summer day. She had an urgent need to curl up in a deep armchair and go to sleep after the early start and lunchtime glass of wine. But a sudden clash of voices from the hall brought her back with a jolt. People were coming this way. She felt guilty, trapped.

She made for the door in the far corner, hoping it was not a cupboard. It opened on to a corridor, dimly lit by a grubby skylight set in the ceiling high above. The lino on the floor was worn and frayed, the hunting prints on the walls heavily foxed. Cardboard boxes were stacked four-high along one side. Obviously not an area intended for public view: left or right?

"Can I help you?"

Clare suppressed a yelp. "I think I've come the wrong way."

"I think you have."

She was approached by a man in late middle age wearing a checked Vyella shirt and baggy grey flannels. He seemed more surprised than annoyed by her intrusion. He looked at her over the top of half-moon glasses, as if studying a form of life hitherto unknown to him. A name badge sagged from the pocket of his shirt.

"You're Mr Ogg," she said. "The churchwarden."

"I am indeed. Both of those things. And general manager of this hotel. But I don't quite see…"

"The rector said I might meet you. Now I see why."

"The rector? You know her?"

"I bumped in to her at St Peter's. She told me

you were responsible for the excellent state of the churchyard."

Valentine Ogg looked bashful. "A slight exaggeration. I merely supervise. But what brings you to a gloomy corridor at Danby Hall?"

"I was exploring and…ended up here by accident."

"Looking for?"

Let's take the bull by the horns, she thought. "My family used to live here. I wanted to see what it was like."

"You must be mistaken, my dear. No family has lived at Danby Hall for many years."

"Perhaps I should have said 'ancestors'. They left in the 1880s, I think."

Valentine frowned and removed his glasses. "The 1880s? That would have been in the Newtons' time."

"That's their name. I found Beatrice Newton's grave in the churchyard. It was rather out of the way."

The churchwarden looked down and said nothing for a few moments. Then he cleared his throat and spoke softly. "There's something you may like to see."

Clare followed him down the corridor, away from the direction of the entrance hall and the residents' lounge, past more boxes and a couple of filing cabinets that had seen better days. On one, an anglepoise lamp crouched low, as if about to strike. On the other, a bakelite telephone, its curly cord dangling over the side.

Valentine stopped by a door and pushed it open with a sharp twist of the handle and well-placed thrust of the shoulder. He stepped to one side and gestured her into the room.

"This is the library," he said. "Or was at one time. It has suffered over the years. I annexed a corner for an office pending restoration of the room to its former glory but somehow that has never been a priority for the limited funds at our disposal. I seem to have spread over the years."

The harsh glare of fluorescent tubes was painful after the murk of the corridor. Clare took in a loose collection of utilitarian furniture and equipment, incongruous against a backdrop of mahogany shelving and gleaming spines. Doors on the far side were blocked by four-drawer filing cabinets a good deal smarter than those outside; yellowing blinds covered the windows at what she assumed was the back of the house.

"Well, at least there are books," she said.

"Quite so. But not the ones that would have been here when the house was lived in. The books and many other objects were removed for safe-keeping during the war and destroyed when a plane came down on the barn in which they were being kept overnight." He shook his head gently. "These came as a job lot from a sale in Suffolk some years ago. Absurdly cheap."

He ducked below a desk and spun the combination lock of a small safe. A brief scrabbling and shuffling of paper produced a manila envelope. He took it over to a more civilised part of the room by the fireplace with a small table, a couple of leather armchairs and an oriental rug. The soft light of a standard lamp provided some relief from the clinical strips overhead.

"These were found under the floor boards when the central heating was being installed upstairs." He slid the contents of the envelope onto the table. "You may like to have a look while I get some tea, Miss Newton."

"It's Mallory. Clare Mallory. Newton was my grandmother's maiden name."

She recognised the hand straightaway. The neat black copperplate of the scrapbook that had belonged to Beatrice. But these few pages were loose, apparently torn with great care from the book currently lying on the kitchen table at number twelve Mulberry Grove. So carefully that she had not noticed anything was missing. This was not the work of a person acting in anger or in haste but coolly and calmly and with great deliberation. Would Beatrice herself, she wondered, have had the strength and control required to remove the pages or was this the act of someone else wanting to hide them from the eyes of others?

It was clear from their tone and content that these pages came from the later, darker part of the scrapbook, shortly before the end. Yet they were more ordered, less frenetic, dominated by a series of sketches of a man gradually transformed into an owl with sharp talons, cruelly curled. And the face, ghostly pale with big black eyes, a face like a mask with a man behind it. The face of a barn owl, by the look of it, roughly the shape of a heart.

Clare felt the chill and shudder she had felt before. Further sketches, almost mirror images of the first, showed the bird turning back into the man. And underneath them the words, 'The owl man screeches. He comes at dusk and leaves at dawn.'

She put the pages on the table and sat back. It was a bit warmer now. From behind the doors blocked by cabinets she heard footsteps, voices. How long had she been sitting here, absorbed and repelled by what she saw? Sketches the more disturbing for the way they had been done, vivid, matter-of-fact, quite different from the cheerful caricatures appearing earlier in the scrapbook. What had prompted the change was far from evident. She wondered about Beatrice's state of mind, whether her illness was more than physical.

She steeled herself to look at the other item that had been in the envelope. It was a single sheet of paper, less than A5 in size when unfolded, with a few short lines in violet ink. The writing was small, rounded, purposeful. The writer was clearly older than Beatrice, probably female, but she did not think it was Sarah. Older than her too; an adult. It simply said, 'She knows. I am certain of it. This must stop directly. If it does not, I am ruined.'

Clare read it several times. It was not a letter. That much was obvious, but whether it was a note to someone or the record of private concerns was as obscure as its meaning. If it had been found with the other pages they were no doubt roughly contemporary but as to the relationship between them and who put them under the floor boards…

A rap on the door broke her train of thought. She let in Valentine Ogg holding a tray with tea and biscuits.

The biscuits they had at case conferences. The chocolate ones she liked.

"The room where the papers were found," he said. "We think it may have been the one occupied in the Newtons' day by the governess, Miss Jeavons. *Ruth* Jeavons, according to my researches. It has a connecting door to a smaller room, possibly the bedroom of the youngest child, Beatrice. We sometimes open up the two and use it as a suite for families."

"She was only eleven when she died, Beatrice. One of those Victorian diseases, I suppose."

"The records say 'consumption' or tuberculosis, as we would call it now. But there's some suggestion that, even if she was ill, it was not the cause of the poor girl's death."

"What makes you say that?"

"Conversations with older residents of Great Danby when I first started looking into the history of the house some years ago. Well before their time, of course, but there were hints, rumours of something more violent. It must have been hushed up for some reason; there's nothing in the newspapers of the period that I could find and no mention anywhere of a post mortem or an inquest."

"No police involvement?"

"Apparently not. The family were, I believe, close friends of the local doctor."

"Who signed the death certificate."

"I imagine so."

"None of which explains what actually happened.

And the family left the house."

"Shortly after Beatrice's funeral. They went to London."

"What happened to Miss Jeavons?"

"I don't know. She seems to have disappeared without trace. I doubt she was local. The rest of the staff would probably have come from round here and may well have stayed in the area."

Valentine drained his cup and said, "Apart from the gardener, Pollard. He left the village to work as head gardener at a house in Yorkshire and never came back. We know this from Harriet Rushton's *Rural Reflections*, published in the 1930s. She was daughter of the rector here in the 1880s – we had one to ourselves in those days. Pollard was supposed to help with the Golden Jubilee celebrations she was organising but departed without a word before the big day."

"When was this?"

"June 1887. The Jubilee was on the twentieth."

The edges of the blinds on the other side of the room shimmered as the late afternoon sun stole through the cracks, throwing lines of bright white light across the floor. Somewhere a phone rang and was swiftly answered. Clare felt her eyelids drooping. But there was unfinished business.

"The note," she said. "And the drawings. Are they from the Newtons' time here?"

"I think so. That's why I thought you might like to see them."

"But who could have done them? Members of the family?"

"Hard to say. The note may be Miss Jeavons herself but what it means and why it was under the floor boards is another matter. It sounds pretty desperate, doesn't it?"

"And the drawings too, in a different sort of way. Weird; haunting. Someone had an over-active imagination." She did not feel ready to mention Beatrice and the scrapbook.

"If imagination it was. Would you care for some more tea?"

"I ought to be getting back. Can I order a taxi to the station?"

"You can but, if you're heading to London, it'll be a two-hour wait for the train. We could put you up here."

Clare faltered. Well, why not? It was more appealing than another microwave meal by herself and Scandinavian gloom on the telly.

She settled into a chair in the bar with a complimentary glass of kir and a copy of the menu, feeling a good deal better – and better about herself – after a short sleep, a shower and a change of clothes. Valentine had arranged it: a visit to Grace and Favour, a rather smart dress agency in the village with a profitable mail order business on the side. The shop had been on the point of closing when she arrived but the name of Ogg was sufficient to persuade Emily Grace to help Clare find something suitably summery at a reasonable price.

She struggled to narrow the first-course options. Potted shrimps, timbale of crab, salmon terrine. Then a voice broke in, clear and confident but not over-confident.

"It's Clare Mallory, isn't it?"

It was a tallish man, early thirties perhaps, with dark brown hair and light brown eyes.

"I'm sorry. I don't think we've…"

"You were at St Luke's; I was at Martlet Hall round the corner. I used to go out with your room-mate, Angela. Paul Barton."

He held out a hand.

"Do you mind if I join you?"

She did remember now. That first term. The rooms she had shared in the main quad, diagonally opposite the chapel. He had emerged, unkempt and bleary-eyed, from Angela's bedroom one Sunday morning on his way to the communal bathroom down half a flight of stairs. He had had a friend, Roger something; she had teamed up with him for a while, each content to accept second-best, as she saw it, in the shadow of Angela and Paul. Things moved on, alliances changed, people went their separate ways. When last heard of, Angela was in New York, working for the United Nations.

By the time they reached the pana cotta, they seemed to have swapped their life stories over the last ten years. She felt more comfortable, more relaxed than she had for a long time. They took a turn in the still-light garden afterwards, settling in the seat with the hint of the Orient she had found that afternoon.

After a while, he said, "I've been put in a room with a connecting door. At the back of the house."

"Really? So have I."

Thirteen

*I*ris had slept badly. Waking with a start in the early hours, cold but sweating, the room a confusion of distorted shapes and elongated shadows cast by the light of a full moon shining through the flimsy curtains. She fumbled for the glass on the cabinet beside her bed and took a sip of water. It tasted stale, dusty, though freshly filled from the kitchen tap before she came upstairs. She turned her back on the window and pulled the quilt about her.

Her mind was racing, thoughts of things done and things undone, opportunities grasped and those let slip, sleights from years long past that made her bristle, bridle even now. And then there was the question of the locket. She couldn't keep it and it couldn't stay here. The only way forward was to meet the girl, preferably on neutral ground, return the locket and explain why she had needed to take it. But how much should she say about what she had gleaned from her readings? This called for some care. The girl was not likely to be receptive, to heed her warnings, if the encounter at the fair was anything to go by. Best to focus on the past and the unfortunate Beatrice and play the rest by ear.

She turned and turned again. It was no good; she was not going to get back to sleep. She reached for her dressing gown – the old paisley one that had been her father's – and went over to the window. She parted the curtains and lowered the sash with a clunk. A sudden scrabbling from the roof. Long pale wings low across the fields, then lost to the woods beyond. Iris shivered and steadied herself against the sill. She gazed towards the horizon, a hint of pink marking the start of another day. Time for breakfast and a proper walk before packing her bag and letting Juno take her home.

She set off along the flinty track, taking the right fork where it divided by the five-bar gate on the boundary of the Brockley estate. She eased over the stile and followed the gently climbing path to Bawson's Clump, a gathering of ancient beeches visible for miles around that had survived the Great Storm of 1987 largely unscathed. Many artists over the years had tried to capture the changing moods and qualities of the clump, few more successfully than the late Nathan Peacock himself. His series of watercolours depicting the woods through the seasons, as seen from Brockley Meadows, had featured on railway posters advertising days out in this part of southern England. Iris had the original artwork framed on her bedroom wall at The Coach House. Not bad for an amateur artist with an undemanding clerical job in local government. It was well beneath his abilities but it kept his head clear for what he wanted to do and kept the wolf from the door in the meantime.

The Peacocks used to trek to the clump from the cottage every spring to see the bluebells in their glory, coming back with armfuls at a time when the picking of wild flowers was not discouraged. She had been back a few times since but not for a while and never alone.

She reached the entrance of the wood warm from the early morning sun and slightly breathless. But as she took the path that wove between the beech, the dense canopy seemed to close in. The smooth grey trunks were immense, confining. It was dark and cold and still, the only sound that of her own heart beating. And then a sudden crash in the undergrowth, a shriek of alarm. She knew she should leave, now. She turned in haste and tripped on a tree root, falling heavily to the ground. As she picked herself up, jarred rather than hurt, she heard the snap of twig and rasp of feet dragging in the beech mast. The chill was intense.

The man was standing between two trees. He looked directly at her. She knew that face, those penetrating eyes. She had seen them staring from the picture in the locket. It was what she had feared. Then he came towards her, slowly raising the sickle he held in his hand.

Fourteen

The junk shop up the hill from Mulberry Grove had recently changed hands. It lay at the heart of vibrant Mulberry Quarter, according to the free magazine she had picked up at the station. Comprehensively Farrow-and-Balled and renamed Verily Vintage, the shop nevertheless retained much of the stock of the previous establishment, supplemented by findings in the markets of northern France and a supply of items picked up for next to nothing at the local auction house of Gavel and Gavel.

It was something to do, she thought, and might even yield a find or two for the house. She decided to walk there, the exercise forming part of her new regime. This initiative, launched with some speed following her weekend at Danby Hall, also involved halving her consumption of alcohol and joining the City branch of Power People, the gym to which Jessica belonged. Whether it was realistic or not to expect these measures to produce rapid results, Clare was feeling positive as she approached the top of the hill, buoyed by the prospect of seeing Paul Barton again when he got back from New York in a week or so.

Paul had told her that he worked for a Cork Street gallery called Bainbridge and Murray. Subsequent late-night googling at number twelve had identified him as a director of the firm. He had apparently been in Norfolk to discuss arrangements for a forthcoming exhibition of new work by Lucy Potter, the latest artist on their books. He promised to invite her to the private view.

A man in a plaid shirt looked up from the racing page and nodded as she entered Verily Vintage. More shabby than chic, she thought, as she wove between furniture in various stages of distress; chipped storage jars empty of *Farine*, *Sucre* and *Sel* posing on shelves of recycled floor boards; heaps of cushions in brand new fabric that would not have looked out of place at the Festival of Britain. Disparate objects with little in common but the inflated figures marked on the price tags.

She brushed past baskets tight with golden grasses, past an alcove boasting kettle and sink, and up the stairs to a small room on the first floor that overlooked the yard at the back. It contained pictures: some on the walls, a few on a table in the middle, most stacked round the room against the skirting.

She glanced at those that could be seen clearly and worked her way through the ones that could not. There seemed little here to detain her. Below the window, face up in a box that had once held bananas, three pictures in identical frames, the glass smeary from a half-hearted attempt to remove the dust. She knelt for a better look. The images themselves were indistinct. But through the glass she made out red initials – NP – in the bottom right-hand corner, each accompanied by dates as illegible as the one on the painting above the fireplace in The Coach House sitting room.

With mounting excitement, Clare lifted the pictures from the box and propped them against the wall. She cleaned the glass as best she could with tissues from the packet she kept in her bag. The paintings, all watercolours, showed rural scenes. One, a clump of tall trees rising above the surrounding fields; the other two, views of a small house in a landscape, much like the picture she had seen before. On the backs of the paintings, their titles inscribed in thick black pencil ('Bawson's Clump', 'Cottage with a Green Door II', 'Cottage with a Green Door III'), were labels for New English Art Club exhibitions many years ago. The name of the artist: Nathan Peacock! And his address: Elder Cottage, Maydown Lane, near Brockley, Hants.

She looked at the pictures more closely in the dazzle of the kitchen spotlights. The man had been only too pleased to see them go, considering the subject matter out of keeping with the retro image he was trying to project. "Fifty quid the lot, luv." They settled on forty. She had carted them back in the banana box and set to work with duster, glass cleaner and kitchen towels. As the pictures gained in clarity, they lost something of their mystery. Yet the more she looked, the more she saw. It was the variety and intensity of the greens that struck her most, complementing and contrasting in shape and tone to produce a harmonious whole. And the play of light and shade on trees and fields, the birds circling the top of the clump (she could almost hear their cries, their caws), the warmth of the cottage brick tempered by grey-white stone. The door of the cottage, at the dead centre of the frontage, like a giant rectangle of baize. The pink dots around it must surely be roses.

Nathan Peacock: Iris's father? The cottage of the paintings could well be Elder Cottage itself. Was that where Iris was now, skulking with her locket? She had to find out. The label said it was near Brockley. It must be the same Brockley – hardly likely to be two in Hampshire – home of Brockley House and not so very far from Oxbourne. She had been to the house once with Jessica, who knew it rather better.

One of the labels had a phone number: Brockley 154. It would not be that now, she thought, even if there was still a separate Brockley exchange. Marigold had said the cottage had no phone, but it would be worth a try. A little internet research confirmed that Brockley numbers had been absorbed by the Easthampton exchange some years ago and prefixed with 723. She stabbed the buttons on her own phone and waited. At least it was ringing. She hung on for five, ten minutes and tried again. Still no answer. Was Iris back or on her way?

Clare walked from the bus stop to The Nook, its entrance marked by two new signs installed by the

Council to replace the ones missing the last time she was here. She wondered how long it would be before they went the way of the others. At the end, she tried the door set within the double gates of The Coach House but it was shut fast. In the absence of knocker or bell, she resorted to tapping then rapping with her knuckles. Before setting out, she had tried the number on the card she had found in Marigold's studio but this time it did not even ring; the line was completely dead.

A rustle and chink behind her. She saw a woman with wild straw-coloured hair dumping two recycling sacks in the road outside the house opposite.

"You must be Mrs Manticore."

"I might be. Who wants to know?"

Clare introduced herself and said, "I was looking for Marigold French or Iris Peacock. Have you seen them recently?"

"I haven't seen that Peacock woman for days. The other one is on the roof. Three sheets to the wind, I shouldn't wonder. I'm surprised she hasn't fallen off."

"On the roof?"

"Flat roof; sort of terrace. They sit out of an evening in the summer. Spying on the neighbours, if you ask me."

"How can I tell her I'm here?"

Mrs Manticore took a step back, cupped her hands around her mouth and yelled, "Mari-g-o-o-o-ld. You've got a visitor."

A high-level head, a wave between the chimney pots. A few minutes later the door was tugged open, with Marigold clinging to it for support. Mrs Manticore slipped away to her own house without another word.

In the sitting room, Marigold confirmed with little prevarication that Elder Cottage was where Iris had gone. Clare went up to the picture above the fireplace.

"May I?"

She lifted it from the wall and turned it over. There were labels similar to the others, the title of the painting: 'Cottage with a Green Door I'. The first of a series but not a series at all. To her eye, they were almost exactly the same. Not like Monet and his haystacks, she thought. Or the front of Rouen Cathedral. Different times, different weather, different light.

Marigold was not much help when the situation was explained.

"Nathan Peacock was Iris's father and had the studio before me. But I never knew him and I don't remember Iris mentioning any other pictures of the cottage."

Neither could she say how the paintings had fetched up in a former junk shop only a few miles away.

"Iris would never have got rid of them. The place means a lot to her. Perhaps it was the sisters."

If she was embarrassed when Clare mentioned the telephone at Elder Cottage, she did not show it. They tried the number using Clare's own mobile. As before, it rang and rang and no one answered. And then the sound of a receiver being lifted and dropped with a crash.

"Iris. Iris. Is that you? Are you all right? Iris."

There was no response, no sound at all. They tried again a few minutes later, but the phone was engaged.

Fifteen

"So," said Jessica. "Tell me about this Paul…"

"Barton," said Clare.

They had made a rare foray into the sitting room at number twelve. The room was warm and stuffy, even with the windows open, and Clare was looking flushed. It was probably the heat.

"Not much to say, really. He recognised me from St Luke's and asked if he could join me. I was glad of the company. We got on. He didn't seem to be trying too hard."

It was, she realised, the first time she and Paul had been together and exchanged more than a few words without the presence of Angela or Roger or both. And the first time he had acknowledged her as anything more than Angela's room-mate. Yet, if things had been cool in the past, there was no mistaking the warmth now. Or so it seemed to her. She wanted to make this one work and, to be honest, it had been a while. Not since she had left the Hornsey flat. Well before that, actually; not since Michael had moved out and in with that hipless young solicitor who had just joined Jessica's firm.

She took a long sip of mineral water and sat back. They were the last to leave the restaurant that night and the staff were getting restless. She could hardly remember what they ate or even what they talked about.

"And then you said goodnight and went your separate ways."

"Turned out our rooms were next to each other. With a connecting door."

"Kept firmly locked by the management."

"It was bolted on both sides. And then it wasn't. We were rather late down for breakfast."

"Hm. Tall, dark and handsome, is he?"

Clare leapt up and left the room, returning almost immediately with her laptop. She set it up on the coffee table and found the home page of Bainbridge and Murray. She clicked on 'Our People' with a practised hand and pointed to the picture immediately below one of the managing director of the firm. Jessica saw a person oozing charm, confidence and quiet authority. A bit too smooth for her taste – she liked a hair or two out of place – and perhaps not entirely to be trusted. It seemed a bit unlikely there no one else in his life. She hoped this wasn't going to end badly.

"Quite a catch," she said. "When am I going to meet him?"

"He's in New York, doing gallery things. I'll let you know when he's back."

*

"What were you doing at a hotel in Norfolk, anyway?"

Jessica was installed at the table in the kitchen while Clare made things sizzle on the hob.

"Danby Hall. It's where Beatrice lived. And died. Her grave is in the churchyard. I thought I'd go and have a look." It was only when she got back home that she wondered whether her room, the smaller of the two, had been Beatrice's once, connecting to the one occupied by the governess, Miss Jeavons. The thought was both exhilarating and disturbing. Had Valentine contrived it as a joke or something more? She reached for a spatula and stirred.

"Any progress on the locket?"

"No – but I've found out the address of the cottage. And, guess what. It's near Brockley."

"What, my Brockley?" She used a tissue to mop up the wine. Brockley House. It was ages since she had been back there, to the Georgian mansion set in parkland in a fold in the Hampshire hills. It was where, delving into the history of her own family, she had first met Duncan, where events were set in train that changed her life. Potentially. So far, the only outward sign was the Camberwell house; most of her money was tied up in investments.

"Yes. Elder Cottage, it's called. In Maydown Lane. Do you know it?"

Jessica shook her head. She pushed back her chair and disposed of the sodden tissue in the bin.

Clare took the pan off the gas and said, "Are you

doing anything tomorrow? I told Marigold I'd try and get down there. Neither of us can raise Iris on the cottage phone so I'm not sure what we'll find."

Sixteen

*I*ris stumbled through the back door and made for the kitchen sink. She filled a glass from the tap and gulped the water down. She stood for a while with her hands on the edge of the sink, staring at the window but not through it. When her breathing became more even, she turned towards the cupboard. She pushed aside items long past their sell-by dates and reviewed the bottles at the back.

Cider: flat; sherry: just a cloudy brown dribble; green chartreuse and grand marnier: been there twenty years at least; cherry brandy: looks OK. Nasty and sweet but it will have to do. She took bottle and glass to the sitting room and slumped in a chair.

The man's face had been deathly pale, the nose beaky sharp, the eyes cold and unblinking. His collarless shirt and open waistcoat were torn and stained. But it was the smell she knew she would remember. The smell of unwashed body, sweat, and putrefaction. She had hauled herself to her feet but she could not run, could not move from the spot. He came closer, sickle held high.

She felt calm, detached as she waited for the fall of the blade. There was nothing she could do.

And suddenly the frantic barking, snarling of a dog, the skittering, scattering of paws on dry twigs and leaves. As she looked away from the man towards the entrance of the clump she heard a loud hiss and a screech. She looked back; the man had gone, the dog sniffing furiously at the ground where he had been.

A whistle and a call. The dog veered the way it had come. Iris was free to move; she walked slowly, stiffly in the same direction. The woods were cool but no longer icy cold.

"Are you all right?" said the woman with the leather dog lead wound round her hand. "You look all shook up."

Iris recognised her as one of the volunteer stewards at Brockley House but could not remember her name. They all looked much the same to her, sitting demurely in their corners, clutching clipboards, biding their time before pouncing on the unsuspecting.

"Yes, thanks. I just tripped over a tree root and gave myself a jolt. I'll be fine."

The woman looked doubtful but did not press. She and her dog made their way, leaving Iris to gather herself in the sunshine before returning to Elder Cottage.

"You're a meddling old fool," she said, pouring another glass of cherry brandy. "You've only yourself to blame."

She stretched to unlace the walking boots she had found under her bed. She kicked them off and went to sleep. At one point she thought she heard the phone ringing but she knew this was unlikely. No one ever rang; no one had the number, apart from Marigold.

It was evening when she finally woke; she had been asleep for hours. She felt thick-headed, dry-mouthed. She was aching with hunger but there was nothing to eat except the remains of a loaf and a softening russet. She had let stocks run down as she was due to go back home. Fat chance. Her tapestry bag lay upstairs unpacked and she was in no state to drive.

The phone rang again. At first she let it ring but it just went on, piercing, insistent. Perhaps she had better answer it, she thought, if only to stop the noise. She eased out of her chair and tottered towards the telephone table. As she reached for the receiver, she fell over one of her boots and knocked into the table. The receiver crashed to the floor. She left it where it was, turned round stiffly and headed for the stairs.

Seventeen

Clare and Jessica set off early. The traffic was light and they made good time. Jessica slowed as they entered the village, neat and tidy and discreetly prosperous, past familiar buildings warming in the morning sun, past the congregation milling in the churchyard of St Giles, past the gold and purple sign that marked the entrance to Brockley House. There were few cars in the visitors' car park – only the grounds and tea room were open at this hour – but she and Clare were not here to see the house.

The table wobbled on the herringbone floor as they pushed their cups to one side and spread out the maps printed, in differing degrees of detail, from the internet. With the aid of Clare's highlighter, they attempted to mark the route from the middle of Brockley to Elder Cottage. This was not straightforward. Maydown Lane was well beyond the confines of the village and appeared to be a track off another track leading from a minor road that wound through the valley of the River Brock.

"Fancy seeing you here, Miss. Making a day of it?"

"Neville!"

Jessica did the introductions. She had reason to be grateful for Neville Filbert's quiet support when she was at Brockley before. They exchanged Christmas cards but she felt guilty she did not come and see him more often. He looked older and had begun to stoop.

"Neville's worked here man and boy."

"And my father before me."

Clare struggled to think of something to say. "We've been trying to work out how to get to Maydown Lane. Elder Cottage."

"That's Nathan Peacock's place. Or used to be. It's been in the family donkeys' years. He did some paintings of Brockley House, you know. In Lady Pamela's day. He presented them to her on her eightieth birthday. They're hanging in the library."

"It's Iris Peacock we've come to see. Clare knows her from London."

"Well, I hope she's all right," said Neville. "One of our volunteers met her coming out of Bawson's Clump yesterday morning. Said she was in a right state and white as a sheet. Looked as if she'd seen a ghost."

The car jerked up the track between high banks enclosed by trees on either side. At the top, the land levelled out to a more open area – and a house. It had no name that they could see but it was clearly a cottage with a green door and there was no other sign of habitation. The track itself petered out at the gate to a field beyond.

Clare got out of the car and looked at the picture on her phone, a photograph of one of Nathan Peacock's paintings of the cottage. The surrounding vegetation had grown abundantly since it was done so that the house was no longer so exposed. And the dip or hollow in which it stood was a good deal less pronounced than the watercolour version suggested. The green of the door in front of her, blistered and flaking in places and faded with the years, was muted in comparison with the miniature she held in her hand.

"Quiet, isn't it?" said Jessica.

Even the sound of birdsong had receded. They took the flinty track at first and turned at the gate. A side view of the cottage gave them sight of Juno and a pile of wood.

"Looks like she's still here," said Clare. "But you'd have thought she would have heard the car."

They walked back along a strip of springy turf bright with scarlet pimpernel. At the front door Clare took hold of the knocker and rammed it hard against the metal plate below. Once, twice, three times. She opened the letter box with a thumb and called out Iris's name and her own.

"We could try round the side," said Jessica.

"No need. Look."

Clare had turned the handle. The door creaked open directly into a whitewashed room with stairs leading off it. The chill was painful after the warmth outside. They proceeded cautiously, uncertain what they would find.

"Iris… Are you there? Iris. It's me, Clare Mallory."

"This place is a tip," said Jessica.

She picked the empty cherry brandy bottle from the rug and put it next to the glass. She gathered the scattered boots and paired them at the base of the telephone table. She retrieved the whining receiver and set it back on the phone. Only then did she wonder whether she should have touched that or anything else.

A thump from somewhere upstairs. Footsteps, shuffling; the creak of floorboards. Clare and Jessica moved closer to the door. A thin voice from the top of the stairs.

"Who's there?"

"Clare Mallory. The door was open. Are you all right?"

Slippered feet gave way to a paisley dressing gown, loosely wrapped. A mottled hand gripped the banister. A creased face, a tousled head. Clare was shocked by Iris's dishevelled state, a far cry from the poise and calm control of Madame Pavonia, famous clairvoyant.

"Put the kettle on, dear. I'll be down in a jiffy."

The jiffy was an extended one, to the sound of running water and movement that was less tentative than before. The kettle had long boiled when Iris appeared, in unexpectedly good spirits, humming a tune with a 'fifties' feel that Clare thought she recognised but could not name. There was no milk left for tea or coffee but they accepted the offer of an infusion of camomile and raspberry. As they sipped in the shade at the back of the cottage, Clare gently raised what

Neville Filbert had reported about Bawson's Clump. Iris brushed the matter aside, citing an exposed tree root; she was fine, thank you, and, yes, she would be all right to drive back to London by herself. All the same, she sounded subdued, the Cockney undertones more pronounced, the theatricality of the tent performance barely a memory.

Iris was not concentrating as she asked Jessica about her work and where she lived. In mid-sentence, she put down her mug with a bang, scraped back her chair and went inside. Jessica took this as a signal to make a strategic withdrawal to the car, ostensibly to make a phone call. Iris returned with a velvet bag. She removed a scrap of bubble wrap and placed it in the palm of Clare's hand.

"I'm sorry you've been parted from your locket, dear. I know it means a lot to you."

Clare unfurled the bubble wrap and suppressed a sob.

"I found it on the floor of the tent. I needed to... understand it before I gave it back. It was easier to do that here."

"Yes, but why..."

"Her name was Beatrice, wasn't it? An ancestor of yours."

"Yes, but how..."

"Do you know much about her, about how she died?"

"Not much. She lived in Norfolk and died young. She was my three-greats aunt."

"And the locket passed to you. Always down the female line."

"My grandmother gave it to me."

"Did she say anything about the locket, about its history since Beatrice died?"

"Not that I remember. I was only twelve."

"You had no trouble with the locket before I… borrowed it? Or anything happening since?"

"Such as?"

"Any unusual events or the appearance of strangers, for example."

"Only cards put daily through my letter box. All colours of the rainbow. You could say that they led me to a stranger."

"Ah, yes. I think perhaps you need a proper explanation. I suggest we meet in London for a talk. Just the two of us. Not a reading; nothing like that."

Eighteen

Sitting with Jessica in the garden of a country pub on the way home from Brockley, Clare unfastened the locket that was back in its rightful place. She opened it deftly and showed Jessica the photograph.

"Does she look like you or do you look like her?" said Jessica.

"Very flattering. She's an eleven-year-old girl dying of consumption."

"The set of her face, the way she holds her head. I can't quite put my finger on it."

"Possibly," said Clare. "Now you come to mention it." She had never previously noticed a likeness. Yet, apart from the dull and vacant eyes, she thought, and the unruly hair, the picture was beginning to resemble photographs of herself at much the same age, examples of which she had seen only recently in her grandmother's box in Oxbourne.

She had taken the locket for granted until it was no longer there. It was not just an object, she realised, a piece of jewellery; it was part of her. Not simply the family history, the fact that she now knew she was related to the girl whose picture and curl of hair were preserved inside it. It was something more, something she had not felt before.

The locket looked the same but was taking on an aura, a character, of its own, intruding Beatrice's life into hers, melding them in some way she sensed but did not understand. Her pleasure at having the locket back was tempered by a growing sense of unease.

When she would have the "proper explanation" of Iris Peacock's abduction of the locket remained to be seen. The ball was in the fortune-teller's court. Having turned up at Elder Cottage unannounced, Clare was reluctant to take the initiative again and, with the passing days, it began to seem less important than it had when the offer was made. She tried to remember what Iris had said in the tent about "P" and why it was supposed to matter. Something about an outstretched hand, was it, about someone who wanted to help? What help did she need? She had the locket now. Anyway, the only P she could think of was Paul Barton. A brief encounter after ten years' absence. Was he still in New York or was he back in London?

She found that she was thinking more about her childhood, her grandmother and the time they shared together. Christmas at Oxbourne, visits to Nutmeg Cottage, the Somerset house where her grandmother had always lived, or so it had seemed to her then. How easy it was to forget that people had lives before you knew them. The pictures now on her phone captured her grandmother in other places, other times, but did not dilute her memories.

There was the week she spent at the cottage, just the two of them, when her brother was ill in bed at home. Her father had driven her there while her mother looked after Colin. She enjoyed the sense of complicity, being allowed to stay up late, the chocolate cake, and having Toby, her grandmother's ginger cat, all to herself for once. It was summer, she recalled, school holidays, and much of the day they were in the garden, lying on their backs in the grass, looking at the clouds moving across the sky. Sometimes slow and leisurely, other times scudding, racing overhead. They saw shapes, faces: a horse's head, a loaf of bread, a cross-looking man, a range of mountains. They used to argue about what they saw. A fish to one was a galleon to the other; a flying saucer, surely crammed with hostile aliens, was held to be no more than a mushroom.

Her grandmother's name was Isobel. She rarely heard it used; she was just Grandma to her. Rummaging in the trunk at Oxbourne, she came across the name, strangely formal, scattered liberally through documents she had not seen before. And on the lid, the letters, yellowed and worn, ISOBEL NEWTON. It was almost like a different person.

The envelope landed with a thud in the hall, propelled

through the letter box with some force, and coming to rest near the bottom of the stairs. She strained to pick it up and take it into the kitchen. Another bad night, kept awake by the screeching and scrabbling that neighbours put down to foxes, though she had never seen them herself. The envelope had a Norfolk postmark. It had been sent from Danby Hall by Valentine Ogg. A brief letter in a neat hand apologised for the delay in sending photocopies of the note and sketches she had seen when she was there and said she might be interested in the photograph enclosed with them. He had had it printed from one of a series of glass plate negatives found in a box behind a disused water tank in the attic. He thought it had been taken in the mid-1880s.

The photograph was a group portrait of the Newton family and their servants taken at the front of the house. With it, a rough tracing outlining the figures and giving the names of those that Valentine could identify. Parents sitting dead centre, looking relaxed and quietly proprietorial, flanked by Augustus and Sarah standing and with Beatrice on a low chair or stool at their feet. How much more cheerful, how much healthier, she seemed than in the picture taken a year or so later. And, on another chair, sitting with the family, yet somehow set apart, a demure woman in a plain dark dress and an expression that gave nothing away. Clare put her age as early thirties, though it was hard to tell. The corresponding name on the tracing was Ruth Jeavons. The governess whose room connected with Beatrice's own.

The indoor and outdoor staff were ranged behind. Her eye passed quickly over the cook, Mrs Holroyd, and sundry maids and came to rest on the man at the end. Thick-set, upright, an air of defiance and a penetrating stare that she found disturbing but strangely compelling. This was Reuben Pollard, the gardener Valentine had told her left the village abruptly before the Golden Jubilee celebrations in June 1887.

She turned the photograph face down on the kitchen table and returned to the letter itself. It had a post script on the other side. Valentine expressed the hope that she would come and see them again soon and said her friend Paul had been on good form when he had stayed the previous week.

Nineteen

Clare was in the garden when the phone rang. She rammed the fork she was using hard into the bed of herbs near the house, crossed the kitchen threshold at speed, and lunged at the instrument on the work surface.

"Danby Hall. That's the place, isn't it? Where you stayed in Norfolk." The line was poor and Jessica's voice was indistinct.

"Yes. But what about it?"

"Duncan bought some books at the auction. At Gavel and Gavel. Four box-loads. Mostly books on art and architecture but with some other stuff too. What they call 'a mixed lot'. They're in piles all over the floor."

"Where does Danby Hall come in?"

"Some of them – dusty old leather-bound things – have book plates. They say 'From the Library of J. E. Newton Esq.'. Then there's a sort of miniature engraving of a house – Duncan is saying it's a bit like Strawberry Hill – and underneath someone has written 'Danby Hall, Norfolk'."

"It must be the same one." What on earth were they

doing among a load of art books and what about the rest of the library? Surely, she thought, the Newtons would have taken all their books with them when they moved to London. The ones Valentine said were destroyed in the war must have belonged to later occupants of Danby Hall.

"We wondered if you'd like to have them. Hang on…Duncan says there are letters or something inside one of the books."

Jessica agreed to come over and pick her up. If she was taken aback at Clare's insistence that she must see the letters straightaway, she did not say so and did not press the point. Besides, what struck her when Clare opened the door at number twelve was how much weight she had lost, even since their trip to Elder Cottage. Especially since then.

"I know. I can get back into things I thought I'd never wear again and nearly chucked out when I left the Hornsey flat. Must be all the exercise and mineral water." She sounded positive but did not feel it. How long had Paul been back? There had to be a simple explanation why he had not been in touch, surely, but she was reluctant to ring him herself.

Duncan was sitting cross-legged on the floor when Clare burst in. He was engrossed by the catalogue of a Sotheby's auction of twentieth-century paintings. The auction had taken place nearly thirty years ago. He raised a tentative head and waved in the direction of a table on the other side of the room. The intervening space was largely covered in books.

"I put them over there."

She was disappointed that there were only three. They were attractive, though, each with gilded spine and marbled boards of varying designs. She sat down at the table and picked up the volume on top: *Excursions in the County of Norfolk: a complete guide for the traveller and tourist, comprising a brief delineation of every town and village together with descriptions of every interesting object of curiosity*. A slip of paper, folded in two, marked the page for Great Danby. A block of densely printed text that she decided to read later; the piece of paper itself was blank, apart from the two words pencilled on the back.

"Duncan. *Duncan*. What does *Tyto alba* mean?"

"Dunno. White something by the sound of it. I'll look it up."

She did not linger over *The Ingoldsby Legends*, not being drawn to stories of ghosts and spectres. The copy of *Evelina* by Fanny Burney held greater interest, less for the book itself than for the sheets of paper – smooth, white, deckle-edged – laid in at the end. She knew this paper, she knew this writing. The same purple ink, the same sensible hand as the note she had first seen in Valentine's office at Danby Hall. The author was the governess, Ruth Jeavons. Had she taken the books with her when she left the Newtons?

Clare was feeling light-headed and slightly sick when Jessica came in with the coffee. She had read the first two sheets with growing excitement but was reluctant to show it. She was too churned up to spend time on explanations and had lost track, in any case, of what she had and hadn't told Jessica about Beatrice, the locket and the documents that had come her way. She hadn't mentioned Miss Jeavons; of that, she was sure. But, even though Jessica was her closest friend and they shared a lot, it seemed better to keep things to herself for the time being. At least until they were clearer and she understood them. She put the papers back inside the book and said she would look at them properly at home.

"Any news of the director of Bainbridge and Murray?" asked Jessica.

"Who?"

"Paul Barton."

"Oh, Paul. Sorry. No, not yet."

"Well, Duncan *has* come across him. Haven't you, Duncan?"

He looked up from the floor, grubby but cheerful.

"Our paths have crossed, once or twice, though not recently. Modern – contemporary – art is his thing. He has a knack of finding 'undiscovered' artists and building their reputations in the market – with the gallery as their sole representative, of course."

"That's what he was doing when I met him," said Clare. "Sorting out arrangements for an exhibition by a new signing, or whatever it's called. Lucy...Potter."

Duncan said he didn't know her, got to his feet unsteadily and picked his way to the door.

"He's going to invite me to the private view," she said in a small voice that went unheard.

*

Duncan returned a few minutes later looking pleased with himself.

"Your *Tyto alba*. It's a barn owl. Does that help?"

Twenty

Clare put the books on the kitchen table at number twelve and removed the sheets from the Fanny Burney. Undated and unnumbered, their timing and sequence were unclear. Some were dense with Miss Jeavons' compact script, others retained broad expanses of white, like the piece Valentine had shown her at Danby Hall. The status and purpose of the entries was also obscure. The loose sheets were not part of a diary or journal, as far as she could see. Nor, given some of the content, would they have formed the basis of subsequent letters. Perhaps they had a cathartic role or were a substitute for the companionship Miss Jeavons craved.

She read through the sheets in the order in which she had found them, angered by some entries, saddened by others. A few were confused and confusing. She pulled a propelling pencil from the inside pocket of her bag and numbered each sheet on the back. Then she reassembled them in the order in which she guessed they had been written and began to read them again.

I have put aside my needlework and taken up the pen. The wind in the chimney has stilled and the house rests quiet. Beyond the doors, young Beatrice lies sleeping. She is a pleasing child and not slow to give affection or to receive it. Her sister remains a little wary and her brother I do not see at all since he went away to school. The girls have started to call me 'Ruthie'. It is a name better suited to the kitchen maid but it is well meant and I take it in good part. I meet my employers when I accompany the girls to see them after tea, but little otherwise. Of my predecessor, Miss Tallow, nothing is said, though I am given to understand that her departure was as sudden as it was unexpected.

My room is tolerably comfortable and I make no complaint about it. My day is spent largely in the school room in the company of children and chalk dust. A little time to myself is not unwelcome but I feel the lack of society in the evenings. Counting the rosebuds in the pattern on my wallpaper does not satisfy.

I had occasion to chastise Sarah for excessive spinning of the school-room globe. Her reply was most insolent. She accused me of treating dear Beatrice as my favourite. I must take care to appear more even-handed.

A pleasant walk with my charges this afternoon, providing fresh air and exercise and a useful opportunity to practise conversing in French. Our pleasure was marred only by the untimely appearance of Pollard, the gardener. I can but be grateful that his look to me went unnoticed by the girls as they sat on the grass making daisy chains. He is a rough sort with a stare like a gimlet that is unnatural and somewhat unsettling. The girls and I collected flowers to press and returned to the school room.

I grow weary of mutton and mashed potato.

At church this morning. The service was well-attended as usual and the singing uncommonly lusty. Afterwards, the Rev Rushton, newly arrived from a parish in Hertfordshire, looked away as I was leaving, a few paces behind my charges, and did not acknowledge me. It is as if I do not exist. I am not one of the family but I am scarcely a servant. I was born a lady, not for my present situation. I am worthy of some respect. Being neither fish nor fowl is hard to bear.

I was given leave by Mrs Newton to take letters to the post office in the village. As if from nowhere, the man Pollard appeared in the street and addressed me directly. I could not follow all his words – the dialect is still a puzzle to me – yet his meaning did not defy comprehension. I bade him good day and went about my business. He laughed, but not as disagreeably as I had previously observed. His labouring makes his brown arms very thick and strong-looking.

A rare expedition to Marsham with Mrs Newton, Sarah and dear Beatrice. I now have a new dress, purchased with the little I have been able to save after sending home money towards the education of my siblings. I have unpicked the lace from the cuffs to make it more becoming. My previous dress was almost in tatters, despite my efforts to keep it in repair.

This does not excuse the glances of the shop girls.

We were looking at the different shapes of leaves in the garden for our study of nature. I stepped behind the yew hedge to make a small adjustment to my clothing, only to be confronted by Pollard. He was wearing no shirt. I did not permit my gaze to linger unduly. He said nothing at first but began to sharpen his sickle upon a stone in a manner that was unnecessary. As I turned to go back to my charges, he commented upon my dress and invited me to call him Reuben. I felt my cheeks redden.

The summer's heat shows no sign of relenting. My charges have little interest in their spelling and arithmetic. As I was opening the school room window to its fullest extent I caught sight of R working in the garden below. I followed his progress for a while until a squabbling between the girls recalled me to my duties. His back and chest, I noted, were as brown as his arms. It is a wonder that he does not have a shirt to protect him from the sun.

Mr Newton has permitted me to make use of his library in what little time I have at leisure. He took pains to explain to me the arrangement of the books and asked me several questions about my reading. He seemed surprised that I was acquainted with the classical authors. I told him that my father had taught me both Latin and Greek. Mr Newton declared a fondness for Pope's translation of the Iliad *but our dialogue was broken short by the arrival of Mrs Newton at the library door. Her demeanour was not altogether friendly. He hastened from the room, but not before saying that I was at liberty to borrow any book that I should care to choose.*

My room is airless and it is difficult to breathe. The curtains hang heavy and lifeless beside the open window. I hear a rasping in the darkness outside but I see nothing. My dear Beatrice tosses and turns in her bed next door... I took my candle and sat beside her. She lay feverish and limp as a rag doll as I mopped her pale brow. Her tangled hair was spread upon the pillow like a fan. I fetched her water but she did not wake to drink it. I left the door between our rooms ajar lest she need me before daybreak.

I dreamed that he came to me. In the half-light, in this room. Such a thing cannot be.

There is a fire within me. It must be extinguished.

My dreams persist. Some nights I hear a screeching in the garden, though it sounds closer. During this last night, upon waking prematurely from my slumbers, I went to the window and thought I saw a silhouette against the moon.

The doctor has been called to my poor Beatrice. It is as I feared. She has asked for a kitten and it will not be denied her. Her people have more time for her now that she herself has less in prospect. The girl spends many hours drawing but she is often unwilling to show me the results. There is no want of affection between us but I detect a knowingness in her manner that was not present before.

Mrs Newton has declined an invitation to join the committee formed to arrange the Jubilee celebration in the village. This is on account of the health of dear Beatrice. It seems that Great Danby is to be made gay with bunting and Chinese lanterns, with many special events and a display of fireworks in the evening. I fancy that the rejoicings will not cross the threshold of Danby Hall.

I learn that Miss Rushton, the rector's daughter, has obtained a part in making the Jubilee arrangements and has recruited R to assist her with certain tasks. I trust she will not detain him over-long.

Poor Beatrice has been coughing most dreadfully and is often fatigued. As she grows thinner my dress becomes tighter, though I eat little enough.

Clare put the last sheet on top of the others and went outside. She sank to a garden chair, still warm from the heat of day, and looked up at the stars, flickering gently in an indigo sky. Poor Miss Jeavons, she thought, the self-consumer of her woes. Fragments of a lonely life, slipped inside a book – or between the floor boards of her room at Danby Hall. It seemed an intrusion, to read her private words, even at this distance. Had others, over the years, seen what she had written, and been affected? Or had *Evelina* kept them safe from prying eyes?

She wondered what had happened to Ruth Jeavons. It seemed unlikely that she would have followed Reuben Pollard to Yorkshire – or been welcomed back by her own family, if Clare's suspicions were correct. Yet the books, those three, had stayed together and been put in a cardboard box quite recently. She must ask Duncan if he knew anything of their provenance.

And then there was Beatrice herself. A lot said in Miss Jeavons' entries, but a lot left unsaid. Nothing about what actually took place, about her sudden death even sooner than the one they had come to expect. The sketches she was reluctant to show her governess, did they include the ones that lay hidden at Danby Hall until disturbed by the central heating men? Clare recalled the words she had first read in the library, 'The owl man screeches. He comes at dusk and leaves at dawn.'

The night had grown chill, clingingly cold. She shivered and went back inside.

Twenty-one

*I*n the privacy of her office on the ground floor of chambers, Clare swapped her sober court attire for something more colourful. Skipping down the steps of Number One Partridge Court, she felt guilty to be leaving before her usual time, even if the place was largely deserted this Friday evening. One of the few remaining, she noticed, was that Romilly Meek, giving her a look through the courtyard window and consulting her watch with exaggerated care.

She picked her way over the cobbles, a painful exercise in brand new shoes, avoiding collision by a hair's breadth with the man in tweeds and bright yellow waistcoat steaming towards her. It was James Daly gripping a briefcase in each hand, as if to maintain a delicate balance. He put them down together and patted his large, pink face with a handkerchief conjured from an inside pocket.

"Long time, no see, my dear. You're looking well, very well. In-deed, yes. What takes you from us in such haste?"

"An appointment...engagement...in the West End. I'm running late. Sorry. Must dash."

The taxi dropped her at one end of Cork Street. Using the window of the Oolong Gallery as a mirror, she brushed her hair and applied the lipstick she had found at the bottom of a drawer last night. Looking more confident than she felt, she headed towards the hubbub halfway down. She wove through the group that had spilled on to the pavement and crossed the threshold of Bainbridge and Murray, a large white cube of light and noise and people. She found the reception desk and presented her invitation to the girl half-hidden by a huge vase of lilies. She was called Dido, according to the sticker on her shirt. The girl chirped a greeting, checked her name on a list, and waved in the general direction of the drinks table. Clare veered towards it, seized a glass of champagne and looked around for...

"Paul!"

He broke away from the scrum and came towards her, looking relaxed in a linen suit. He kissed her on the lips and said,

"Great to see you again."

"How was New York?"

"Busy. A lot of useful contacts but too many good lunches."

"Been back long?"

"A little while. I meant to get in touch sooner. I've been tied up with last-minute arrangements for the private view. Things I thought had been sorted out in my absence."

"Hm. Which one is Lucy Potter?"

He took her over her to a woman with shortish hair, dyed bright orange. He made the introductions and left them to it for a few moments. The artist was standing at the point in the gallery where new works – semi-abstract scenes of East Anglian coast and countryside – gave way to a wall of older paintings in a quite different style. These ones were not for sale.

"They're supposed to show the development of me oeuvre," said Lucy. She pronounced it to rhyme with 'hoover'. "I haven't seen most of them for years." She pointed to 'A Street in Bodrum' and 'Sunset over Zonguldak' hanging in the middle. "These two have a sense of menace and time suspended reminiscent of de Chirico, according to the man from the *Standard*. Isn't that right, Hugh?"

"Hugh" turned out to be Hugh Mullion, the 'private collector' who had lent the paintings. He wasn't paying attention, distracted by the two small girls who had run giggling into Cork Street with a plate of samosas. He put down his glass and pursued them.

"His daughters," said Lucy, as she finished Hugh's champagne and was led away to meet a reporter from the BBC.

Clare wasn't sure about another glass but she put up little resistance when Belinda – sister of Dido at reception, Paul said – came round with a tray. She turned to the wall of East Anglian scenes. All pretty muted, but for the red stickers already spreading across the captions like a rash. 'Church in the rain' and 'Winter trees' had a melancholy air that 'Sea mist: dawn' and 'Willows by the creek' did little to dispel. 'Reeds in early morning light' struck a more cheerful note, as did 'Figures on a beach', but the overall impression was subdued, with a predominance of greys and browns and silvery greens.

And then she looked again. A stripe of yellow ochre on the bark of a tree, a sliver of apricot reflected in water, a smudge of rose pink on the distant horizon. The more she stared the more the pictures increased in depth and definition and came to life. She took a few steps back, just avoiding the toes of the man with the small black moustache talking to Lucy. He was introduced as Anthony Buffo, a south London bookseller who also had an interest – "for historical reasons," he said – in a gallery in New York.

"It's called The New Romulus Gallery. I'm rarely there these days. My daughter Caroline runs the place. She met Paul Barton when he was there a little while ago, showed him round. I'm told they got on like a house on fire."

"Oh, really?"

"Purely business," said Lucy, perhaps a little too quickly. "Caroline bought some of my pictures once when she was in London. At an exhibition in Anthony's bookshop. So, you see, she already knows my work. The New Romulus is going to handle things in New York on behalf of Bainbridge and Murray."

"Ah."

"Lucy and I were talking about photography," said Anthony, taking an extended sip of champagne. His forehead was gleaming under the spotlights. "Or, rather, I was asking her if she ever painted from photographs, if only as an aide-mémoire."

"That would be cheating and it wouldn't work anyway," said Lucy. "Not for me. I paint what I see, not what a camera records. To see something properly you need to be there and absorb it. A painting isn't just the click of a lens. A camera doesn't engage with its subject or interpret it in the same way. I draw and sketch for ages. Sometimes hours just standing or sitting in the same place. The finished painting is the scene as it is through my eyes and with all my baggage."

Clare half-turned towards the wall. "Yes," she said. "I can understand that. They say the camera doesn't lie but it's an odd kind of truth if it doesn't represent what you actually see." She looked at the pictures in silence for a moment and then said to Lucy, "That one at the top. On the far right. It looks familiar."

Her memory of the meal afterwards was hazy. A Japanese restaurant somewhere in Mayfair five minutes' walk from the gallery. There were six of them at the beginning: Clare and Paul, Lucy and Anthony, and another couple from the private view whose names she may have been told.

Lobster and sea urchin were involved somewhere along the line. Of that, she was fairly certain. Tuna and sea bass may also have been implicated. Whose idea it was to sample the bewildering array of sake was less clear. Eventually, it was just her and Paul, though she had no recollection of the others departing. There was a taxi and a panelled lift with doors like a concertina. And, as she told Jessica a day or two later, he really did have some etchings to show her, not that he lingered long over the drypoints before moving to other business.

Twenty-two

*W*hen the exhibition was over, Paul brought the picture round himself and helped her put it up. 'The Harbour, Sanderling': black-boarded fishermen's huts, roofs sharp against a pale grey sky barely distinguishable from the sea, dull yellow beach in the foreground, sliced by groynes stepping down to the water's edge. It was not one of Lucy's more colourful paintings but, for Clare, a reminder of the afternoon she and her father had been there in search of Colin, her brother, when he had gone missing without a word. Colin and "that girl", as her mother put it; Clare felt a bit more sympathy for him now.

Sitting in the garden later, she mentioned to Paul her conversation with Lucy about painting and photography.
"Yes," he said. "The camera changes what you see and how you see it. All our catalogues are on-line and we produce videos to go with some of them. We think the quality is pretty good but it's never the same as the real thing. You lose the feel and texture of the painting

when you see the image as a whole and you lose the context if you zoom in on particular parts. You may see the details better but it changes the relationship with the rest of the painting."

"Like postcards. Even if they have the ones of the pictures you like, they're flat in comparison with the originals and the colours are never right. And they're completely the wrong size, of course. Reproductions aren't really reproductions at all, are they? More like versions."

"Some are better than others but they're never more than approximations. You need to see the originals to appreciate them properly but that's not always possible so prints and posters and postcards have to do. And they're a bit cheaper too."

She topped up Paul's glass and said, "I gather you know Duncan; met him, anyway."

"Duncan who?"

"Duncan Westwood. He's a…friend of *my* friend Jessica. He teaches art history and has written one or two books."

"The 'animals in art' man? I have met him."

"Well, he picked up a whole load of art books and catalogues at an auction. I saw them at Jessica's; he had them spread all over the floor. Some of them are quite old and colour printing has come on a bit since they were published. Duncan was looking at one and saying that none of the pictures gave any idea of what the artist intended and that hardly anyone now understood them in any case."

"Why's that?"

"He meant that most people don't get the classical or biblical references these days, the allusions and the signs and symbols."

"True but that's why there are experts around to interpret them."

"Do you have to understand a painting's original purpose or meaning, what the artist intended, in order to appreciate it?"

"Not necessarily, though you may get more out of it. The aesthetic value is independent. And we each see things in our own way, depending on our background, experience, interests, etc."

"So if we each see a slightly different painting perhaps it doesn't matter whether it's the original or not."

The following day, they ambled down Mulberry Grove to The Golden Goose. It was Sunday lunchtime and there was jazz upstairs. Playing today, the Dave Sutcliffe Quartet, according to the poster on the board outside. The name meant nothing to her but Paul spoke highly of them, having heard the band a couple of times, he said, late at night at Ronnie's Bar. The room on the first floor was a large one, covering the entire footprint of the pub, with a low stage at one end, a bar at the other, and a scattering of tables and chairs in between. Makeshift curtains across selected windows kept out the brightest of the light on a cloudless day.

A mixture of standards and new pieces, said Dave

Sutcliffe, pressing a hand to his pork-pie hat as he hopped to the stage with an alto sax. He introduced the other members of the band with a sweep of the arm, names Clare failed to make out above the ribald remarks of supporters lounging at the front. She could at least see their instruments: keyboards, drums, double bass. First off, Dave's own arrangement of that old Jerome Kern favourite, 'A Fine Romance'. She pretended not to notice the knowing glance from the neighbours at number ten.

As the set progressed, the gentle murmur from the bar area was punctuated by the loud conversation of new arrivals, men who had already had a few downstairs, she guessed. Heads turned, people shushed.

"Well, well, well. Look who it is."

A red-faced man swayed towards her, dripping a trail of lager. She did not know him. But she recognised the pair skulking behind. It was the youth with the mobile phone she had seen outside Madame Pavonia's tent at the fair – and Gary Parslow, looking no more confident than he had that day in court.

"If it's not Perry Mason. Or should that be his grand-daughter?"

The rim of his glass caught the light from the stage, looked sharp, threatening. She moved her chair closer to Paul's.

"Who?"

"Before your time, son. It's her all right. The bint that humiliated our Gary over the van, sliced him up and had him on toast."

"Come away, Dad."

"Seen the future, have you?" The man stepped up to the table. He loomed over her and brayed, "Was there anything there? Eh? Eh?"

"Let's go, Dad."

He brought down his glass with a bang but backed off as Paul rose and the others pulled him away.

"You can't ignore us, Miss High-and-Mighty. We know where you live."

Clare shifted in her seat and tried to look unconcerned while the men were ushered out to the street by the manager and Paul went to get her something stronger than mineral water. She had promised to explain things to him later but had not decided how much to say. She was too churned up to think much beyond the confines of The Golden Goose. They *did* know where she lived. But why would they do anything about it now? They had had plenty of time in the weeks since the cards and flyer came through the letter box. The encounter in the pub was fortuitous, she reasoned, the words fuelled by alcohol. On the other hand, it would do no harm to be vigilant in public places, to keep the chain on the front door when she was at home.

Excursions in the County of Norfolk. She had put it with the other two books and Miss Jeavons' papers in the filing cabinet in the study. After Paul headed back to his Kensington flat, she retrieved the volume and took it downstairs to the kitchen table. She had told him she would be fine on her own, was used to it, but she was beginning to feel apprehensive about being alone in the house.

Excursions, she read, was published in 1824 and illustrated with a map and seventy-five engravings, according to the title page. As she leafed through the book, glancing at views of ruins in fields, windmills on ridges, grand country houses, she came upon a dried flower, squashed flat and drained of colour. An insubstantial thing, almost translucent. She could not identify what flower it had been before it was plucked and pressed and hidden from view. It seemed best to leave it where it was, where perhaps Miss Jeavons herself had placed it in her lonely room at Danby Hall.

She turned to the page marked by the slip of paper, folded in two. There was no engraving or other decoration, just a block of text following the entry for Great Barnham:

GREAT DANBY, a village of some antiquity lying rather more than four miles to the south-west of Marsham. It was formerly known as Danby Magna to distinguish it from Danby Parva, or Little Danby, in the county of Suffolk. Entering by the Marsham Road, the traveller's attention is arrested by the fine tower of the church, dedicated to St Peter. The interior of the building is remarkable chiefly for the marble tomb of Sir John Danby, whose arms may be seen in the lower corners of the north window. The Danby family resided in the old manor house, a mediaeval structure once located near the church but long since destroyed. The present Danby Hall, the seat of Ralph Paxton Esq, is of altogether more recent construction and a deal less considerable, to judge by local account. The hall was built on Ebbett's Field, the site of an annual horse fair and achieving some renown in the county as the place at which Martha Pollard and two others were apprehended on a charge of witchcraft and sent for trial at Norwich Assizes in 1646.

Martha Pollard? She steadied herself. It could well be a common surname in that part of Norfolk. She put the slip of paper back in the book. The two words in pencil caught her eye. *Tyto alba*. A barn owl, Duncan had said. She thought again of the sketches Valentine Ogg had first shown her at Danby Hall and of what was written underneath them: 'The owl man screeches. He comes at dusk and leaves at dawn.' If there was any connection, she could not see it.

The light was failing fast, the birch trees at the end black against the remnants of a flaming sky. The rest of the garden was already lost in gloom. Clare checked that the glazed doors were locked and wished they had blinds or curtains or some other covering. She remembered to put the chain on the front door, then went upstairs to close the windows before returning to pour herself a drink and send an e-mail.

Twenty-three

This time Valentine was expecting her. He was pacing the reception area as she clambered out of the taxi from Marsham station, paid the driver and hastened in to Danby Hall. He relieved her of her overnight bag, shook the rain off her coat, and handed both to a loitering member of staff. They went through to the lounge where coffee and miniature Danish pastries were waiting.

"I've done some research," he said, wiping sticky fingers on a paper napkin. "Consulted various parish and county records with the assistance of an archivist friend of mine. It seems that Martha Pollard was accused of entertaining evil spirits, along with one Elizabeth Farthing and a Mrs Bradshaw. Quite how this was manifested is unclear but the suggestion is that their confessions were 'encouraged' by starving them and depriving them of sleep for days and nights on end. They were all hanged."

"That's awful," said Clare. She had scanned the page from *Excursions* and Miss Jeavons' documents and e-mailed them to him a couple of weeks ago, explaining how she had acquired them and asking him if he could shed any light on Pollard's namesake. She felt a sense of complicity with Valentine on matters linked to Beatrice that led her to confide in ways she was not yet ready to do with Jessica or Paul. It was answers to her own questions she wanted. "Those women were tortured."

"Just part of the mania for rooting out supposed witches in those days, I'm afraid, especially in East Anglia. Their crime was probably no more than having a squint or a scolding tongue or keeping a cat. Or just getting on the wrong side of the neighbours."

"Did you discover whether she was related to our Pollard…to Reuben?"

"Martha Pollard was a widow by the time of her own death. Her husband had been the local hedger and they had two children: a son and a daughter. Reuben, it seems, is a direct descendent through the son, who was also a hedger. There were Pollards in the village for centuries. Right up to the time Reuben left: he was the last of a long line."

"The last living in Great Danby. Didn't you say he went to Yorkshire? He could have had a family there, or somewhere else if he moved on."

"It's quite possible; I've no idea what happened to him."

"He was in the photograph you sent me, the one of the family and servants – and Miss Jeavons. You marked his name on the tracing."

"I did."

"How did you know it was him?"

"He was the gardener. No one else in the picture answered that description."

"When I was in Great Danby before, in the churchyard trying to find Beatrice's grave, I saw a man with a sickle. It was only a glimpse, and I can't be sure, but when I looked at the photograph again last night I thought there was a likeness I hadn't noticed earlier."

"Doesn't sound like anyone around here. I know just about everyone in the village. Besides, no one uses a sickle in the churchyard these days."

A fresh cafetière arrived to replace the first. Clare declined Valentine's offer of another Danish pastry and said, "I was wondering. You don't suppose Pollard and Miss Jeavons were…"

"Lovers?" he said, with a directness that surprised her. "The governess and the gardener? Not in the 1880s. It's unthinkable. It would have been instant dismissal for them both, if they'd been found out."

"They both left pretty quickly – and about the same time."

"True. But that was after Beatrice died. Anyway, think of the logistics. She spent most of her time with her charges and most of what little remained in her room. With Beatrice next door. There's no question of Pollard being allowed in the main part of the house, let alone in the governess's bedroom."

"The tone of Miss Jeavons' diary, journal, whatever, suggests more than a professional interest in the gardener."

"The fantasies of a lonely young woman, I fear. I don't see how anything could have come of it."

"Not even a clandestine visit, at night while Beatrice and the rest of the family were asleep."

"Incredibly risky and I still don't see how it could have been done. The room is on the second floor. There's no way of climbing in and there wouldn't have been then."

"Ladder?"

"Not at that height and difficult to do without making a racket in the dark."

"*Tyto alba.*"

"I'm sorry?"

"It means barn owl. The words were written on a piece of paper marking the Great Danby page in the Norfolk book. I wondered if there was any connection with Beatrice's drawings, the ones you showed me last time."

"There could be. But which came first? Maybe they just saw an owl one evening in the garden and one thing led to…"

"Mr Ogg. Mr Ogg." A youth burst in, red-faced, breathless. "It's the Reverend Virgo. On the phone. She says it's urgent."

Valentine rose apologetically and followed the youth to reception. A few minutes later both he and Clare left the building and drove the short distance to St Peter's church. The Reverend Virgo hovered beneath the lych gate.

"Vandals," she said, with a nod to Clare as she led

them through the churchyard, keys jangling at her belt. Valentine's golfing umbrella was a colourful addition to a dull grey day but ineffective as a means of shelter as he struggled to control it in the growing gale. Stepping over puddles, and dodging the spokes of the umbrella, Clare barely glanced at the tower of the church, the one described as 'fine' by the author of *Excursions*.

It was drier under the yews at the end of the path.

"Look at that," said the rector. "Who on earth would have done such a thing? And why?"

Clare fought back the tears as she knelt to examine the remains of Beatrice's shattered grave. The small headstone had been wrenched from the earth and lay hacked and chipped against the leg of the bench nearby. The image of the dove, she saw, was largely obliterated. On the back of the stone, a series of frantic scratches showed ghostly white through the lichen.

"The work of a wild beast," said Valentine.

"Or a mad man," said the rector. "Mad *men*, I should say. No one person would have had the strength to uproot a gravestone. Even one this size."

Clare stood up and took a few paces back. As she did so, the scratches began to resolve into letters, the letters into words.

"Look. It says something. 'There…is…no…peace'. 'There is no peace'."

"'For the wicked'," said Valentine.

"There is no peace, saith the Lord, *unto* the wicked," put in the Reverend Virgo. "Isaiah 48:22. The King James version."

"I'll fetch a tarpaulin to cover the grave. I suggest we rope off the area for now and then decide what to do."

"I thought the rector would want to call the police," said Clare, warming herself against a radiator. The hotel's central heating had been put back on unexpectedly early, summer's lease having a while to run.

"She may yet do so but I see some advantage in trying to keep this low-profile, if we can. If parishioners ask, we can always say the grave collapsed, the ground was unstable, or something. None of the other graves was touched."

"I'll pay for the damage to be repaired. And a new headstone – exactly the same as before. I have some pictures of it on my phone."

"Let me have a word with the rector. There's a firm of monumental masons in Marsham who may be able to help. I'd be happy to contribute, given the Danby Hall connection. But don't we need to be sure this won't happen again?"

"Beatrice's grave can't stay like that."

"Not long-term, certainly. Leave it with me."

"I was wondering," said Clare. "Has anything else happened since I was here before?"

"Such as?"

"Any unexplained events, appearances, noises, for example?"

"Not that I can think of. The occasional vulpine screech from the garden in the early hours, but that's not unusual. Oh, and the family we had in the suite on the second floor. They complained that their daughter had seen a face at the window. Nonsense, of course, at that height; it was probably her own reflection."

The rain relented after lunch and a weak sun emerged. As Valentine had hotel matters to pursue, Clare walked in to the village, having seen little of it beyond the limits of the churchyard. The dress agency was closed and there were no other shops apart from a general store in the former corn and seed merchant, a faded sign still evident high on the front of the building. Of the post office mentioned by Miss Jeavons there was no trace, just a V R box set in a wall between The Old Forge and Saddler's Cottage. The Old School House a few doors down was just that: Great Danby National School built in 1844 and since converted to residential use.

She came back along the Marsham Road. It had begun to steam, the sun now shining brightly, the remaining cloud wispy as a streak of smoke or a lock of hair. She recalled Valentine's reaction when she unclipped the locket at table, flipped it open and shown him the photograph inside.

"Sorry," he said, having failed to disguise a start of surprise. "For a split second I thought it was you. Obviously impossible. Silly of me."

Pretty much what Jessica had said too, only more so. A family resemblance was to be expected. They were related. But Clare knew it was more than that. She had noticed the growing likeness before but, sitting with the locket next to Valentine, she could see that the similarity was striking. And not just to Clare as she had been at much the same age as Beatrice but as she was now. The hair was still unruly but the eyes were no longer the dull and lifeless features captured in the valuation details safe in the filing cabinet at number twelve. The unease that had been with her these past weeks was growing too.

On the other side of the road, The Black Horse, Great Danby's remaining pub, loomed on rising ground, a few parked cars gleaming outside. Further on, there was an area of grass, freshly mown, lying within sight of St Peter's and doing duty as the village green. She crossed and sat on a bench close to the war memorial placed in the middle. A catalogue of Great War losses. So many, she thought, from a village that, even then, could not have had more than a few hundred inhabitants at most. It was the recurrence of the surnames that she found most upsetting. Two, three, sometimes four of the same name. Husbands, fathers, sons, brothers. In the column nearer Clare: Lightning, Manship, Medlar, Newstead, Pardon, Pilgrim, Ogg.

Twenty-four

She had some misgivings about staying in Beatrice's room again. Her overnight bag had been taken there when she arrived and unpacked while she was still downstairs with Valentine. It seemed churlish to ask to be moved, particularly as she was staying at a heavily discounted rate. In the event, the night passed quietly enough but her mind was churning too much for sleep before the early hours.

She had broached the subject of the war memorial that evening during the main course. T A Ogg, Valentine said, was his great-uncle, Thomas Arthur Ogg. He had worked briefly at the grocers in the premises now occupied by the dress agency before being sent to France. It was the first time he had left the village, and the last. He was killed at the Somme in 1916 and the family moved to Norwich. No Ogg had been back to Great Danby until Valentine took over the failing hotel, then called The Pines, and the place reverted to its former name of Danby Hall.

Clare was on the point of asking if he had always

been there by himself but sensed that it was a subject better avoided. Instead, she said, "So, you had Paul with you the other week. Paul Barton." She gave a high, nervous laugh and gulped down her remaining ration of wine.

"Yes, indeed. Most convivial. I joined him after his artist friend had left – the one with orange hair – and he told me about his trip to New York. Never a dull moment, by the sound of it. Particularly the incident at the oyster bar at Grand Central station with someone he knows at the UN. I gather the stain came out all right."

"Someone he knows at the UN."

"Yes, makes us seem very parochial in Great Danby, doesn't it?"

"Would this someone be called *Angela*, by any chance?"

"Er, I don't think he mentioned the name."

Angela. Angela Meadows. She should have made the connection, the pair having been inseparable for much of the time at St Luke's. It wasn't his college but you wouldn't have known it. He had shown no interest in art or artists in those days, as far as she could remember. Acting was more his thing. Martlet Hall reviews in the garden of the Master's Lodgings. Pimms beforehand on the lawn, a makeshift stage under the awning strung between two Judas trees. Paul playing the comedy Yorkshireman. Exaggerated, of course, but he had still had the trace of an accent then. Now you couldn't tell at all.

*

She slept fitfully, her head a torment of anxieties and ill-formed thoughts. She was used to being independent, in charge, in control, but she felt her grip loosening, her life increasingly prey to events, chance findings and initiatives taken by others. Outside the office, at any rate. At work, she still managed to immerse herself in the cases to hand and there was nothing to suggest that clients or colleagues noticed any change in her performance or powers of concentration.

Her suspicions about Angela could be unfounded. Why shouldn't he look up an old flame when he was in New York? He probably hadn't seen her for years. And Caroline Buffo simply ran the gallery handling things for Bainbridge and Murray. Naturally they would have dealings; it was part of the job. She knew all this really but logic was in short supply in the early hours. Paul had been good to her, and good for her, she conceded, but the nagging thought persisted that he might be stringing her along.

On her way back after breakfast, Clare had to pass the adjoining room before reaching her own. The previous occupiers had already left and the door was ajar. A chariot piled with clean towels and bedlinen was parked outside but of the staff there was neither sight nor sound. She glanced along the corridor and stepped into the room. Miss Jeavons' solitary domain. She had been there before, that night with Paul, but not by herself and not since she had read the poignant passages written in secret in this room. Regency stripes had replaced the rosebud wallpaper, fitted carpet covered the floorboards. But as Clare looked round, she could imagine an iron bedstead hard against the wall, a table and chair by the cast iron fireplace, a modest chest of drawers and a wash stand with jug and bowl. No bath or shower room in Miss Jeavons' time.

She crossed to the window and stared into the garden, forehead pressed against the glass. For a moment, she thought she saw a man working below, dead-heading flowers past their first flush, tying back straggling stems. A noise from the corridor made her turn and when she looked back the man was no longer there. Perhaps he had gone to find a shirt for the air was still cool at this hour despite the makings of a fine day.

The chambermaid was unbothered by her exit from the wrong room. They exchanged good mornings and Clare swiped into the room next door to re-read the pages of neat purple ink she had brought with her.

Twenty-five

"Duncan only went and left a box behind," said Jessica.

She and Clare were having coffee in the kitchen of her house in Camberwell.

"Another box of books?"

"Yeah. It got muddled up under a table with a separate multiple lot, apparently. Guess who had to go to the auctioneers to collect it."

"Why you?"

"Well, he's back in north London, preparing for next term's course on German Expressionism. Gavels were threatening to start charging if the box wasn't picked up."

"Hm." Got things nicely organised, hasn't he, thought Clare. The house was fast becoming a repository for Duncan's purchases. Maybe Jessica should charge for storage too.

"The box weighed a ton. A porter put it in the boot for me but I had to cart the books into the house in batches. It took ages and I was filthy by the end of it."

"Anything of interest?"

"More of the same: art books and old catalogues. As if he didn't have enough. Oh, and that." She pointed at the item lying on the dresser. "He hasn't seen it yet."

"May I?"

Clare picked up a large black volume with rubbed corners and a worn leather spine, banded in gold. As she opened it, endpapers like watered silk shimmered seductively in the morning light.

"It's a photograph album," said Jessica. "Pictures of an old house called Tarleton Lodge. The name's written inside."

Clare turned the pages slowly. Many were foxed but the sepia photographs centred on them, singly or in pairs, were unblemished and sharp. They were views of a sizeable house, perhaps early nineteenth century, set in its own grounds. Several had captions in careful copperplate confirming the name of the house and the particular parts on show.

She saw rolling lawns, neatly kept and punctuated at intervals by urns and circular flower beds; extensive greenhouses; a lake fringed by trees and shrubs that were reflected on the surface, the water crowded with ducks she could imagine quacking gently as they went about their business. A welcome relief from the formality of gardens that were strangely bereft, she thought, of any sign of human life.

And then, finally, a picture of three youngish women, not dissimilar in appearance, posing in front of rampant shrubbery that could well have been rhododendron bushes. They were attempting to look serious, but not too serious, and none was able to conceal a mischievous sparkle in the eye. Underneath, the initials E, A and C.

"Do we know who they are?"

"Not a clue," said Jessica. "They look quite genteel, don't they, as you might expect in a house like that. I don't know where the house is either."

They were interrupted by the telephone, chirruping in its cradle by the door.

"It's Duncan. I'll take it the sitting room."

Clare continued to stare at the photograph for a while, looking for connections, clues, anything that might suggest a link: the box was from the same lot as the others. The following pages were blank, the rest of the album empty but for an unused postcard of a steamer on the Rhine and a piece of paper inserted near the end. As she removed it, her hands were shaking. She felt like she used to before exams or interviews. The paper itself was different, as was the ink, but she recognised the writing straightaway.

It is many months since I left Great Danby and since I last set down my thoughts. To my eternal regret, I was unable to attend the funeral of poor Beatrice, taken from us so horribly. My position in the house had become insupportable and I had to go. I hastened as best I could to catch the morning train to Marsham and reached the station breathless and scarcely able to ask for my ticket. The station master, Mr Kettle, helped me to the carriage with my bag. To my shame, I did not return the books to Mr Newton's library, or leave them on the table in my room, but perhaps he has not noticed a few missing among so many.

R departed the village with no word to me. Where he went I do not know. I have no expectation that I shall see him again and no longer a desire to do so. If he had cared for me, as I once supposed…

I feared that I should be obliged to put up at a boarding house in one of the less salubrious areas and endeavour to take matters from there. It is my great good fortune that Emily and her sisters were able to accommodate me at their Streatham home with discretion and forbearance. A testimony to the strength of the friendship of years past and, it is to be hoped, of many years to come. Before too long, when my health has returned, I shall have to make my own way but the sisters do not press and seem keen for me to stay. There is even talk of establishing a school for young ladies. How I shall repay their kindness, and that of Dr Salmon, in making arrangements at some risk to themselves I have yet to determine. We are of a mind that it was for the best in all the circumstances.

From my window, I see the blossom of horse chestnuts along the roadside and the glint of sun reflected on the surface of the lake. The garden was given over to celebration of the Jubilee shortly after my arrival last year. There was quite a throng and a deal of merriment by the sound of it. I did not participate myself but Emily's sister Allegra thought to bring me oranges and nuts and a gingerbread man from one of the stalls. They sustained me for several days afterwards during the hours that sleep eluded me. My own thoughts were on Great Danby and the bright new penny that dear Beatrice had asked me to give to Miss Rushton for her collection towards the Queen's Jubilee present. I still have it, wrapped in tissue paper, in my chest of drawers. A small memento of a life cut short even sooner than her expected term. I do not believe that the poor girl suffered at the end, it was so quick. Such is my fervent hope. Would that I had acted with greater caution…

Clare was reading Miss Jeavons' note a second time when Jessica came back into the kitchen. It was too late to hide it, to slip it into her bag or between the pages of the album. She said nothing as Jessica approached the table, did not even look up. She simply held out the note and started to cry.

Twenty-six

Re-reading it at home for the umpteenth time, the note Miss Jeavons had written at Tarleton Lodge seemed to Clare more measured, more level-headed than the Danby Hall fragments. But it also seemed more detached, more matter-of-fact in a way that she found unsettling. And it pretty much confirmed why the governess had had to leave Great Danby in a hurry.

Miss Jeavons' habit of hiding notes inside larger volumes had ensured their preservation but did not explain why she had put them there in the first place. Where had they been for the last hundred years or so? Had they really remained undisturbed all this time? Yet if they had been seen by other eyes, they would surely have been removed and probably destroyed. She must ask Duncan again if he knew where the books had come from; they had been boxed up fairly recently, presumably, for sale at the auction itself.

With Duncan's blessing, Jessica had let her have the photograph album as well as the note inside it. She had given Jessica some account that day of Beatrice, her untimely death, and the lonely life of her governess, Ruth Jeavons. How much more she had said in her tearful state she could not remember. She would have said something about the previous documents that had come her way, if only to make clear how she had recognised the writing of the latest one to surface. As to Pollard, she did not elaborate, professing ignorance of the identity of 'R'; neither did she refer to the desecration of Beatrice's grave in Great Danby or to the more disturbing drawings that the girl had produced in her final months. She needed some secrets and she claimed Great Danby largely as her own. She wanted to keep London and Great Danby apart as far as she could but the connections seemed only to grow stronger. Besides, she disliked speculation and preferred to keep her suspicions of past and present to herself, at least until things were clearer: beyond reasonable doubt rather than a simple balance of probability.

Perhaps Iris's promised explanation might shed some light on more than the fortune-teller's own motives in taking the locket. Somehow, she had known that the picture inside it was of Beatrice. She had said at much at the cottage but not how she knew and Clare had been too focussed on the return of her locket to follow the point up at the time.

The more pressing issue, however, was to reassure Jessica that her failure to take her friend into her confidence earlier indicated no more than that the loss of the locket, and discoveries about Beatrice, had affected her more than she had realised or could rationalise. Jessica stood by her in any event.

The local on-line archive confirmed that Tarleton Lodge had been located not so very far from Mulberry Grove; it had been demolished in the 1920s to make way for a London County Council housing development, known as the Tarleton Estate. That was still there but Clare had no desire to see it, preferring to think of the place as it had been in Miss Jeavons' time. A series of historic maps in the archive confirmed that the grounds of the Lodge had been extensive, even in comparison with other large houses in the area.

The website had an engraving of the house in 1820, standing sedate beyond the fence that bordered an empty country lane. It was described as the residence of Hartley Neville Esq; there was no information about later occupants of the property. However, further googling unearthed an article about the house in the proceedings of a local history society. It mentioned that it was the home of three sisters, the Misses Woodward, for many years. Census records confirmed that Emily, Allegra and Charlotte were in residence when Ruth Jeavons must have joined them and remained so until the house was demolished. The oddity was that there was no reference to Miss Jeavons living at Tarleton Lodge in any capacity. About a school for young ladies, the records were silent.

According to Duncan, the catalogue said nothing about

the provenance of the books he had bought or of any of the other books in the auction. He suggested that his boxes were the result of a house clearance, probably after someone had died.

"So some of the other lots could have come from the same place," said Clare.

"It's quite possible but the multiple lots at least all sold so they'll have been dispersed. No doubt bought by dealers. I didn't look at them closely as I was interested in the art stuff, even if some other things found their way in."

"Gavels is only two or three miles from where you said Tarleton Lodge used to be," said Jessica. "So your Miss Jeavons may not have moved very far."

"Funny to think she may have lived somewhere near me. Anyway, she must have died a very long time ago. Probably well before the war."

Twenty-seven

Those who heard it spoke variously of screeches, shrieking, and unearthly cries. A clerk from Boswell Buildings, crossing the car park on his way to the bike racks, saw the flash of metal in lamplight. The man from Rummage Court said that the smell was "absolutely appalling…like rotting meat or worse". James Daly himself was unable to give a coherent account of events, then or later. Yet an attack had clearly taken place, his jacket ripped, his waistcoat slashed, before the assailant made off ("simply vanished into thin air") as others ran to his assistance. Raised like a shield in a rapid reflex action, his bulging briefcase had borne the brunt of the assault, subjected to a frenzy of slicing and hacking that left it in shreds and destroyed much of the contents.

James Daly had had a narrow escape. And perhaps Clare too. She had been with him a few minutes beforehand, waylaid as she came back from court, until she made her excuses and slipped to chambers.

The motive of the attack was assumed to be robbery, there being no other rational explanation. Yet nothing was taken. James Daly had no more than two days off, before returning to work with his arm in a sling and wearing a brand new waistcoat. His colleagues declined the offer to look at his stitches.

The talk at Partridge Court the following day was of little but the incident on the other side of Middle Temple Lane. James Daly's spirited defence had earned him a new-found respect and the sniggering parodies quietly dropped, at least for the time being. Some spoke of an owl having been seen in the branches of a plane tree close to the scene, looking down at the injured Daly and the remains of his case. Although reported to the police investigating the incident, they considered it of limited relevance to their inquiries, apparently, the shape of the blade used by the attacker proving to be of greater interest.

Clare found it hard to keep her mind on her work. She convinced herself that she had been the intended victim and that James Daly had paid the price for diverting her from the path she would have taken, thereby frustrating the assailant's plans. The man with the sickle she had seen in the churchyard, the face at the window reported by Valentine, the smashed headstone with the frantic scratches, and now an attack in her own territory, in the middle of London. The idea defied all logic and explanation but she was taking no chances. With the nights drawing in, she was reluctant to linger late at Number One. Unable to share her suspicions with other members of chambers, who would scarcely have believed her in any case, she felt the burden of her isolation. The attack at least provided a plausible excuse for going home earlier. Even Romilly Meek seemed apprehensive. The trouble was that, if Clare was right, there was no reason why she should be safer anywhere else. As she well knew. Any lingering threat from the Parslow clan was surely insignificant by comparison.

Twenty-eight

*I*t had been Paul's idea to go. He was always on the lookout for new talent, he said, and it might be worth a try. Anthony Buffo had put him on the list after meeting him at Lucy Potter's private view. Clare had had an invitation too but had been reluctant to trek over to a second-hand bookshop in a part of south London quite unknown to her. On the other hand, the offer of a lift in Paul's new car on a Saturday that he happened to be at Mulberry Grove put a different complexion on the matter.

Toad Books – second-hand and antiquarian books bought and sold; collections purchased – was roughly in the middle of a parade flanked by a betting shop and a smart new bakery that had taken over the premises of the former off-licence. Paul parked round the corner in Costard Street.

The bookshop was warm and welcoming and smelled of freshly brewed coffee. As they looked round for the pictures, a piercing wolf whistle split the air. They saw a parrot on top of its cage near the window.

"Sorry about Charlie," said the mousy woman who rose from the cash desk. "He's an African Grey, you know. He'll outlive us all." She introduced herself as Marjorie and pointed to the doors to the right of the shop. They opened on to the gallery area, a bright white room in which a few people were circulating, nursing cups of coffee and looking at pictures. Among them, a woman in black hissed to her companion that pictures twice as good could be picked up at half the price at the monthly auctions at Gavel and Gavel.

Marigold's exhibition had been put together in some haste to fill a gap after the person scheduled to do the textiles and embroidery dropped out with glandular fever. Clare recognised the fish on a blue plate – the label confirmed that they were mackerel – centred on the wall ahead and already sold. The pictures were mostly still lifes that struck her as competent but fairly dull. There were a few landscapes, including a couple reminiscent of her watercolour of Bawson's Clump, and, on one wall, a group of portraits from an earlier phase.

It was dominated by a picture (not for sale) of a brown-haired woman with a vase of peacock feathers. It was Iris! She looked years younger, her features taut, her eyes clear and bright. She was gazing away from the viewer at some distant point beyond the picture's frame. Around her neck, beads of deep turquoise and pale celeste brought out the colours of the feathers looming behind her.

"She was here last night," said Marjorie, bringing cups of coffee for Clare and Paul. "She came with

Marigold French. Between you and me, she wasn't looking too well."

Clare left Paul looking at the pictures with far greater care and attention than she could muster and wandered back into the body of the shop. She felt guilty about not getting in touch with Iris even though the onus had been on Iris to contact her. Perhaps she had been ill, in view of what Marjorie had said.

Not keen on being heckled by a parrot, Clare followed the sign that said 'More Books Upstairs'. She climbed slowly, taking in the theatre posters placed at regular intervals on the wall next to her, sipping coffee as she went. At the top, two rooms on the left, doors open, lined with books from floor to ceiling with more ranged on tables in the middle. The first 'Poetry, Plays and Performing Arts', the second 'Travel, Sport and Gardening'. Along the right, piles of boxes the length of the corridor, far outnumbering the ones stacked outside the library at Danby Hall.

As she was about to go into the first room to look for another copy of the Larkin she had lent and never got back, the door at the end juddered open. A man appeared. It was Anthony Buffo.

"Clare Mallory," she said. "We met at Lucy's private view."

"So we did." A look of mild distraction gave way to one of recognition. "And I dimly recall a Japanese restaurant afterwards, though how I got home I'm not sure. Whose idea *was* the sake?"

"No one is admitting to it, though I have my suspicions."

"Have you come to see the paintings?"

"We have. Thanks for the invitation. I left Paul downstairs."

"Not quite up to the standards of Bainbridge and Murray, I'm afraid. A bit of a mixed bag, if you ask me. Marigold French has been badgering me for some time and stepped in at the last minute. Still, it brings people in and some of them buy books too."

"You've a lot to sell," said Clare, nodding towards the boxes by the wall.

"I must stop going to auctions. I allow myself to be tempted by the multiple lots. They're shamefully cheap when you think of the number of books."

She felt her cheeks redden, her stomach tighten. She gulped down the last of the coffee and put the question.

"Do you go to Gavel and Gavel?"

"Far too often. Six boxes from the last sale," he said with a mixture of pride and regret. He patted the box on the top of the pile nearest him. It had a small label, not unlike a raffle ticket, saying '500'.

After a couple of false starts, she explained why she would like to have a look at the latest boxes. At a better time. If it wasn't too much of a nuisance. Paul, clunking up the stairs to find her, had been keen to help. He was not so keen on taking Marigold on to his books but thought he might include a few of her better paintings in the Christmas show by way of a trial run.

It was left that they would come back when the shop closed and take Anthony out for a meal afterwards.

"Bring some old clothes," he said. "The books are thick with dust."

"What exactly are we looking for?" asked Paul. "And where do we start?"

He and Anthony had created a large space in the poetry room by moving the table to one corner. They lugged in the boxes one by one. It was clear from the labels that they comprised two lots: 500 and 501. Clare had a vague idea that Duncan had bought 502. How many multiple lots were there? Perhaps Anthony had the catalogue to hand. He had retreated downstairs with a bag of parrot mix and some corks for Charlie.

"Any books that don't seem to fit with what's in the rest of the box, such as age or subject matter, or have something slipped inside – or anything else which gives a clue about where they might have come from. Or isn't a book at all," she added, thinking of the album of photographs of Tarleton Lodge.

They removed all the books from the first box, flicking through each one, then repeated the process with box number two. Volumes with an ownership signature, bookplate or prize label were set to one side, as were those with postcards, envelopes and any other insertions of interest. The rest were put straight back. Three boxes in, Anthony appeared with cups of coffee, looked at the pile accumulating under the table, and went to try and find the catalogue.

Clare and Paul paused to take stock, legs stiff with crouching or kneeling on the floor. The books so far were a mixture of history, biography, travel, a smattering of English classics, and novels by people they had never heard of, once popular perhaps but long since forgotten. And nothing that had been published in the last twenty or thirty years, by the look of it.

She hobbled over to the window and stared through the grubby glass, over the forecourt of the parade below and across the road to the solid Victorian houses on the other side, their rose-red faces glowing in the dying moments of the day. Yet it was the stillness that struck her. There was no sound, no movement, a brief hiatus between the homeward rush from the shops and the flurry that heralded a Saturday night out.

She tried to imagine who had owned the books. What sort of person had assembled such a disparate collection, taken with the ones that Duncan had bought? What did it say about the life he or she had led? Somehow a he seemed more likely, she thought. What of the circumstances of its dispersal? Had there been no one to pass the books to, no family, no friends? And where did Ruth Jeavons fit into the picture?

A sudden cough or clearing of the throat. She looked back into the room and saw a man pointing to his watch. For a moment, she wondered who it was. Then she walked over to the switch by the door and turned on the light and they moved on to box number four.

The remaining boxes yielded more of the same, apart

from a small collection of classical authors in Latin and Greek and some obscure works of theology that looked to Paul as though they had never been opened. Dreary things, he thought, even if the bindings were more attractive than most of the others. He was in two minds whether to put them back. He was tired, hungry and wanted a drink. But, with Anthony hovering at the doorway and Clare working frantically through a cache of her own, he decided to keep options open and add them to the mound under the table. For simplicity, he tossed on the last book in the box, *Nature's Bounty or The Outdoor World for Boys and Girls*. It had a gold stag beetle on the cover.

There was no way they could sort through the pile before going to the restaurant and no way they would want to tackle it afterwards. Anthony suggested that Clare looked at the books at her leisure at home and made no comment about the quantity that had been set aside. Dismissing any notion of payment, he helped Paul box them up and put them in the boot of his car.

"Keep anything you want and let me have the others back some time."

Clare and Paul washed away the grime in the kitchen at the rear of the bookshop and changed into something cleaner. Charlie was in his cage making short work of a champagne cork. Anthony told him where they were going and they set off. It was only a short walk to Le Chardon Bleu, a bistro in the next parade.

Clare was subdued as they shared a heap of

charcuterie, served on a large piece of slate set between them.

"I'm not sure what I thought we'd find," she said. "I'll make a start on our haul tomorrow. I would have expected something a bit more recent: fiction, anything. And there were no paperbacks at all. Not even any old Penguins."

"Pity," said Anthony, spearing a gherkin with his fork. "They're quite collectible these days. I found the catalogue, by the way. As I thought, there were just the three multiple lots: the art books and the ones you've just seen. Everything else was in ones and twos. I suppose Gavels might have held some back for the next auction."

"Oh no," said Paul. "Don't say that."

Clare managed a weak smile as she reached for a slice of saucisson sec.

"The next auction with books, that is. That'll be in a couple of months or so. Of course, if it was a house clearance, as seems likely, there's no reason why it would have been confined to books. It could have been the entire contents."

She went back to bed after Paul left in the morning. Still leaning against the skirting, on either side of the bedroom fireplace, the pictures she had bought at Verily Vintage, the watercolours by Nathan Peacock. She couldn't decide where to hang them, or whether to put them on a wall at all. Paul had liked them but they didn't really belong here. The cottage was Iris's domain, part of her family history. Marigold had said it meant a lot to her. Perhaps she should let Iris have the pictures. But did Iris need three near-identical versions of 'Cottage with a Green Door'?

The other one... what was it called again? She slid from under the quilt and turned the picture round. The title 'Bawson's Clump' in thick black pencil. She turned it back and held it in front of her. Tall trees rising high above fields, birds circling black against the sky. It was, she realised, the place that featured in one of Marigold's landscapes. The same place, yet utterly different. Marigold's routine rendering conveyed none of the majesty and mystery of Nathan's painting, the sense of the clump as a spot better avoided. Perhaps it was the isolated group of trees she had seen in the distance, beyond the flinty track, when she had been to Elder Cottage. Her mind had been on other things.

She shivered and felt uneasy, fearful. The room had become chill, despite the growing heat of the day. She saw a face reflected in the picture's glass, a face not unlike her own but gaunt and lacking life. And, for the briefest moment, she thought she saw another face, in the space to the right of the head, the face of a man with staring eyes. They were staring at her.

Clare blinked and the man was gone. The other face in the glass was restored to health. She turned the picture against the wall but the image of the man stayed with her. She knew who it was: how long it would be? She wished that Paul was still here.

Twenty-nine

*I*t was difficult to know where to start. She was crouching over the box she had pushed across the floor from where Paul had left it last night. A pleasant warm breeze through the open door, the distant creak of a trampoline, children's voices, the scrape of chair on paving.

She dipped in with both hands and brought books to the kitchen table. She did not recognise them or remember why they had been set aside. They must have been ones Paul had selected. She flicked through them, trying to avoid the distraction of the subject matter, focussing on any oddities or insertions or other things of interest. An unused postcard of Pissarro's painting of Lordship Lane station, a third class train ticket to the same station (it had surely closed years ago), an advertisement for surgical stockings, a label recording the award of the book (*Hakluyt's Voyages*) as a prize for diligence and regular attendance.

She wrote the details of school, recipient and date in her old St George's exercise book, the dragon on the cover inked in neatly with purple felt tip. The names recorded meant nothing to her but, she thought, they might recur, build up a picture, point her in the right direction. As for the other items, each no doubt had its own story to tell but they did not help her with the provenance of the books or offer any obvious connection with Miss Jeavons.

Piles on the table, hands grey with dust. She started to sneeze uncontrollably. She sniffed over to the roll of kitchen towel by the sink, then washed away the grime and went outside. Two feathers, soft, pale, speckled, floated to her feet. She recognised them as ones she had blown off her bedroom window cill that morning; they must have been caught in the gutter, she thought, and dislodged by a draught of air.

The sun was now on the back of the house and prickingly hot. She flopped onto the grass in the quivering shade of silver birch. Swifts were wheeling high in the sky above, next door's water feature splashed gently beyond the fence.

The box was nearly empty. She had notes, names, addresses, some in south-east London, others further afield. No clear pattern was emerging. She had been certain there would be more than a random assortment of cards, leaflets, tickets, wrappers and empty envelopes. Was there something she had missed? Perhaps she should work through the books again once she had disposed of the remaining few. She felt drowsy in the summer's heat, could so easily have succumbed to sleep. But she had to get on, had to complete the task.

Books on theology with darkened spines and bright gilt edges. More of Paul's selections. Why on earth had he picked these out? They were so tight in their bindings they would hardly open. There were no labels or anything slipped inside; just initials pencilled faintly on the flyleaves. RJ, RJ, RJ and then in full, Robert Jeavons. *Robert* Jeavons? Ruth's father, brother? Only one had a publication date and that was in the 1860s.

Her mouth was dry, her cheeks flushed. She knocked over the box as she grabbed at the books that were left. She brought up some smallish volumes, bound in leather and discreetly decorated. They were obviously a set, or part of a set, of classical authors: Herodotus, Homer, Catullus, Ovid, Virgil... . Each had a bookplate, the same bookplate. None said 'Danby Hall, Norfolk.'. They did not need to; she recognised the engraving of the house straightaway. And, as if to resolve any lingering doubt, the words: 'From the Library of J. E. Newton Esq.'.

Surely, Miss Jeavons could not have walked off with these as well. Apparently not, for, inside the Homer, there was a short letter, though no indication of where it had been sent:

8 Ashley Villas
London W
15 May '03

My dear Ruth,

It was good to meet you in the park after so long and looking so well. The years have been kinder to you than they have been to me. Please accept these volumes with my compliments. They have given me much pleasure and I know that you will appreciate them.

With kind regards to you and your family,

Yours ever,

James Newton

Family? She said it out loud, almost shouted. Ruth was married after her time at Tarleton Lodge? Or was he alluding to her parents or siblings? The more she delved into the past, the more questions were raised. It was answers she wanted. The books had obviously been kept together until someone, presumably a descendant, had died or been forced by circumstances to relinquish them over a century later. The idea was rather upsetting. Perhaps she had been meant to find them, to save them from oblivion, along with the others unearthed by Jessica and Duncan.

She needed a drink. There was some wine left in the bottle in the fridge. A dull rattle as her foot caught the edge of the box. She had thought it was empty but there was one book left. The stag beetle on the cover, gold on a dark-blue ground, gleamed in a low stab of sun through the open door. She had last seen one in the garden at home in Oxbourne. Years ago now. It was skulking by the wood pile near the compost heap. Colin was poking it with a stick until she intervened, coaxed it on to a trowel and set it down away from harm.

Nature's Bounty, she read, *or The Outdoor World for Boys and Girls*. It was heavy with illustrations in the text, interspersed with coloured plates of butterflies and moths, birds and their eggs, wildflowers and grasses. The book stayed open of its own accord at the place marked by a small manila envelope. It was the section on birds of prey. Her eye was drawn to the passage about the owl, a bird rebuked by the author for its nocturnal habit, silent and stealthy movement, and mournful cry. 'A creature giving rise to fears and superstition', it said, a little above the ghostly figure of a barn owl.

She reached for the envelope and turned it over. The postmark was indistinct but the stamp bore the head of the present Queen. Neither name nor address tallied with those in her exercise book. She recognised the street as one a short bus ride away, largish houses just off the common. The name on the envelope was Martin Pollard.

*

She downed the first glass and poured another, her regime of relative restraint temporarily suspended. She felt taunted, manipulated, the butt of an elaborate joke. It was almost as if she were the one being sought out, drawn in. Yet, for all her sense of being the natural custodian of the things she had found, there could have been no way of ensuring or foretelling that she would come across them. It was pure chance. Even the books yielding finds had been picked out by other people.

She made her way, a little unsteadily, to the sitting room and put a CD in the player. It was an album by the Dave Sutcliffe Quartet, bought by Paul that afternoon at The Golden Goose in an attempt to further her appreciation of jazz. The music was soothing, gentle, made it seem later than it was. She curled up on the settee and put a cushion on her feet. She was in no hurry to loosen the pink ribbon round the brief for tomorrow that was crammed into her case in the hall.

Martin Pollard. Could *he*, she wondered, have been the last owner of the books, dying without offspring or anyone else to leave them to? Or maybe relations, friends, whoever, were satisfied with the more recent books conspicuous by their absence in the boxes she had seen. Or perhaps, as Anthony had suggested, they were simply being held back for a later auction.

That Martin Pollard was a descendant, possibly grandson, of Ruth and Reuben seemed scarcely credible. Yet she could think of no other explanation. The note in the photograph album had suggested that Ruth no longer wanted to see Reuben; he had surely gone to Yorkshire anyway. On the other hand, if he had found out where she was, re-established contact, shown he cared for her, her real feelings, never fully extinguished, could have been rekindled.

Pure speculation. Some of it could be checked in the records now that she had more to go on. But getting this far had been more demanding, draining than she had realised. She felt exhausted. The re-assertion – and perpetuation – of the Pollard connection disturbed her, as did the entry on birds of prey bookmarked long after Ruth and Reuben must have died. She needed to take stock, get things into perspective. Then she could decide what to do.

Thirty

*P*aul left his overnight bag at the bottom of the stairs at number twelve and went straight out again, leaving the door on the snib. Clare had sent him to buy cod and chips from the Neptune fish bar at the other end of Mulberry Grove while she had a restoring shower. They had been to a drinks party in the gardens of Partridge Court, hosted by head of chambers Gordon Russell, to celebrate Jeremy Wicken-Fenn's achievement in taking silk at the age of thirty-five. Despite his comprehensive sampling of the range and quantity of canapés on offer, Paul claimed he was starving by the time they reached the house.

Clare was feeling apprehensive as she put plates to warm in the oven before going upstairs. They were off to Oxbourne in the morning, the first time she had presented a boyfriend to the parents in quite a while. Her mother's relentless questioning about his background, interests, career prospects and dietary preferences had left her in two minds about whether to go at all.

A sudden click outside the sliding doors. The garden was bathed in brilliance as the security light flashed on, bleaching everything a ghostly white, the colour of old bones. She peered through the glass but could make out nothing. The light went off again. Beyond the spillage of the kitchen spots the garden was now in darkness. And then a screeching and a scrabbling of the sort that neighbours had said was caused by foxes. Yet it seemed too high, the noise, coming from the trees or roof ridge or even from the air between them. The mildness of evening had turned a bitter cold.

What made her open the door, she did not know. She took a step on to the patio; perhaps it was two. The light snapped back on, casting out the shadows. There was a figure on the lawn, a man, standing still, staring at the ground. Slowly, he raised his head and threw her a look, a look of pure malevolence, fixed, unblinking. He made to come towards her. In his hand, she saw the curved blade of a sickle, the sharp edge gleaming. She screamed but no sound came; her mouth was dry, her throat was tight. She tried to turn, to leap the short distance to safety. But her legs would not function. She was fixed to the paving beneath her. He came closer, bringing the blade higher, then higher still. A stench of sweat and putrefaction stung her eyes and nose. She felt weightless, helpless, the strength drained from her. All she could do was wait.

Paul sauntered up the path swinging the bag from the fish shop and pushed open the front door. As he shut it behind him, he was struck by the chill and the silence and the glow of light coming from the kitchen, or through it. He called her name, once, twice. He dropped the bag and ran into the kitchen. He saw her outside, standing motionless – as if turned to stone, he said later. A man pacing towards her, almost mechanically, filthy clothes, disgusting smell, about to cut her down with a curved blade raised above him. The man seemed unaware of Paul forcing wide the intervening door, his shouts, his frantic attempts to drag her back. A look of loathing, contempt, focussed on one thing only.

Shoving her to the wooden bench at right angles to the door, Paul grabbed the garden fork from the herb bed and lunged. The clash of metal on metal brought the man to consciousness of a sort. He faltered but did not retreat, his stare a mixture of fury and surprise. As he lifted the blade again, Paul stabbed wildly with the fork. It struck home – arm, shoulder, he wasn't sure. An unearthly shriek and hissing as the man staggered back. Paul turned for an instant as Clare let out a low moan and whimpered on the bench and as quickly turned again. The man had gone.

She had recognised him, of course. The man she had seen in the churchyard at Great Danby, the man in the group portrait that Valentine had sent her, standing at the end of the back row. Reuben Pollard. He was even wearing the same clothes. It was what she had feared after the attack on James Daly. What had brought him back, she could not say. She guessed it was linked to

Beatrice, that the man was determined to mete out the punishment suffered by that poor girl. But it did not explain why he should have come after Clare, regarded her with such hatred and contempt.

Lying on the settee with Paul, though, dipping into a shared bag of chips, she felt curiously calm, relaxed, as if a great weight had been lifted. She was barely aware of the bruises where he had knocked her to the bench. There was no point in dwelling on what would have happened if he had not got back in time or if she had not left the fork stuck in the herb bed. She knew the answer well enough. He had, she had, and that was that.

Paul was rather less relaxed. Relieved as he was that she was relatively unharmed, he found her composure hard to fathom. She had very nearly been hacked to death by a madman. Why would she not let him call the police? How could she possibly say that the man wouldn't strike again? If not her, then someone else?

"Trust me," she said. And, yes, she still wanted to go to Oxbourne in the morning. Explanations, she told herself, could come later. For now, she just wanted to curl up and go to sleep.

Thirty-one

"You had a narrow escape," said Iris. "You and me both."

They were sitting in the shade of a large umbrella on the flat roof of The Coach House. Marigold had brought them iced tea and withdrawn to her studio, leaving Peevish heaped under a chair. An e-mail to her chambers' address had suggested the meeting. Iris said she was sorry about the delay, she had not been well, but Clare wondered whether its timing was entirely coincidental.

"It's my fault. I should never have interfered. I knew the locket held danger but the forces were too strong for me to resist or control. My meddling nearly cost us our lives."

"Why did he hate so much?" said Clare.

"He was a troubled soul. We had disturbed his peace, such as it was. He held us responsible. I brought him back, you had the link with Beatrice herself. A living reminder of a life cut short. That he cut short."

"Perhaps she was just in the wrong place at the wrong time, had seen and threatened to tell."

Iris shrugged. "Either way, we'll hear from him no more."

Clare unclipped the locket and opened it.

"The photograph," she said.

"It's as I remember it."

"Exactly. But Beatrice had begun to look like me. That's not my imagination; other people also noticed the similarity. Even the lock of hair had begun to get darker, more like mine."

"He thought you *were* Beatrice, not just her descendant?"

"I don't know but, when I opened the locket a day or two after the attack, I saw that the photograph was changing back. The hair too."

"The forces were more powerful than I thought," Iris said softly. She looked tired, drawn.

"An ancestor of Pollard's was tried as a witch. In the seventeenth century. They hanged her."

"Poor woman. But what does it prove?"

"I was wondering if there was something he could have inherited, passed down the generations."

"Such as?"

"An ability to change form, perhaps. To make it easier to come and go without being seen."

"The idea is an ancient one but surely confined to myths and stories, folklore, the supernatural."

Clare hesitated, then reached for her iced tea and took a long sip.

"You were nearly right when you said I had no future."

"I said that I *saw* no future, my dear. Not strictly true but I was working to a brief. They wanted me to give you a fright, to unsettle you without doing any real harm. They're not violent types."

"But why? What I had I done to them?"

"Grayson v Parslow. Gary Parslow is Joan's boy; my nephew."

"I remember the case. I remember him." And the incident in The Golden Goose, Gary hovering, embarrassed, behind his father. "I was representing Sonia Grayson."

"They felt you were...a little hard on Gary, humiliated him in public, so to speak. 'Crucified,' they said. He's not a confident boy at the best of times."

"It's nothing personal. Surely they understand that. It's my job: to get the best for my client. Gary had his own Counsel."

"I've told them enough is enough. From what I hear, it was threatening to get out of hand. You won't be bothered by the Parslows again. Joan will see to that. I think we can safely call it quits. Even I didn't foresee quite how things would turn out."

A bit of an understatement, thought Clare. She said, "Well, I did meet P. He was rather more than 'a helping hand': he saved my life."

It was cooler downstairs. They were in the sitting room, Clare on the settee, Iris on a balloon back chair covered in plum velvet. In the lull after talking about Paul, Clare was looking at a small picture above the fireplace, a watercolour of a cottage with a green door.

"NP," she said, pointing to the initials in the bottom right-hand corner. "Marigold said it was your father, Nathan."

"A gifted amateur," said Iris. "We were brought up on the smell of paint and painting – oil, gouache, but mostly watercolour. The conservatory was his studio, just as it is Marigold's now. It still seems funny to have it back in use after all these years." She paused and said nothing for a while, her gaze focussed on the jug of flowers in the hearth. Then, looking up, "The cottage and the countryside around, those were his first love. We never went abroad; holidays were always there when we were young. He used to paint for hours, often the same thing. He said each one was different but we couldn't see it."

Iris eased herself up and beckoned Clare to follow. They climbed the stairs to her bedroom, a light and airy room, overlooking the courtyard. Iris squeezed past the end of her bed, a large double with a sequinned cover, and hovered in front a mahogany chest of drawers. On the chest, a black-and-white photograph of a man standing in front of a door, framed by roses; above it, a portrait of the same man in oils, with the familiar initials and a date in the corner.

"My father in the late 1950s," she said, taking in both with a gentle sweep. And in both a tallish man, a double-breasted suit, high forehead, kindly eyes, the trace of a smile. They reminded Clare of the portrait of Iris herself, the one she had seen at Marigold's exhibition.

"Looks a nice man," said Clare. Not just for something to say; she meant it.

"He was, and as I remember him best. He didn't change much at all, not until the last years. *They* were his," she said, turning to the wall with four large pictures of woods through the seasons. From the clear light and bluebells of spring to the frosted bleakness of winter.

"Bawson's Clump."

"Quite right. A commission from the Southern Railway, on the strength of a picture shown at the Summer Exhibition. I knew the place well, years ago. We all did."

"Who was Bawson? A local farmer?"

"No, no. Bawson is an old word for a badger, like brock. A badger features in the Brockley coat of arms, you know."

She did; she decided then and there to give her own picture of the clump to Jessica. It was the least she could do.

As if on impulse, Iris went back to the chest and pulled open the top drawer on the left. Clare caught a glimpse of scarves, silk and chiffon, as Iris fumbled and poked around.

"Not there," she said to herself and tried the one on the right. She removed a piece of paper and delved again, bringing up a long, flat box with a tooled leather top.

"I feel I owe you a little more than an apology," she

said, flipping the clasp with a forefinger and presenting the open box to Clare.

Looped inside, the string of beads of deepest turquoise and pale celeste that she had been wearing in the portrait by Marigold.

"I don't have a daughter and you'll appreciate it more than any of my sisters' brood. Let's try it on." She moved Clare's locket to one side and put the beads around her neck.

"They suit you," she said, turning Clare gently towards the mirror on top of the chest. "Your hair, your colouring."

"Thank you" was all Clare could manage for the moment. And then, "They're lovely."

Iris picked up the sheet of paper, the printout from the chambers' website, and held it beside the mirror. The picture of Clare was barely distinguishable from the reflection in the mirror.

She folded the paper in two and dropped it in the bin.

"We won't tell Marigold about the beads. She might not understand."

Clare wrenched the *Borough News* from the letter box of number twelve and took it through to the kitchen. She flicked through it while waiting for the kettle to boil. The usual collection of robberies, muggings, traffic accidents, visits to the area by minor dignitaries. At the bottom of an inside page, a brief article about a dead owl found the previous week lying by the boating lake in her local park. It had been injured, caught by a fox or a feral cat, the paper suggested, possibly after flying into overhead wires.

Thirty-two

The stonemasons in Marsham had done a good job. A new headstone set in place, a measure of dignity restored. Clare read the words, freshly cut in smooth, unweathered stone, that she had first seen above a scattering of nettles in the shade of a yew:

BEATRICE NEWTON
1876 – 1887
She fell asleep too soon.

Beneath the words, the image of a dove. It was bearing, she now realised, a small olive branch in its beak. She bent to straighten the vase of apricot roses she had placed on the grave. The roses had been snipped that morning from the garden at Danby Hall, the vase offered by Valentine Ogg from a selection in a cupboard in the pantry.

"Rather affecting," said Paul, as she took his arm and

they snaked between the other graves in the direction of the south porch. They had spent the night at the hotel as guests of Valentine, with whom she had shared the costs of the headstone. Valentine himself had been subdued that day, had declined to join them at the grave-side. He had shown an unexpected coolness when she had confided in the garden her discovery of an envelope with the name of Martin Pollard, slipped inside another book from the auction. She was puzzled, thought he would be keen to hear what she had to say. But, in the circumstances, she did not elaborate. The roses he passed her were placed in the trug in silence.

Paul had squared things with the neighbours when they asked about the noise – the shouting, the clashing of metal – apologising for watching a DVD of *Spartacus* too close to the open door of the kitchen. He did not press Clare further about the incident, for the time being, and went along with her assurance that the books they had taken pains to sort had yielded nothing much of interest. "So far. I'm going to go through them again when I have a moment."

He had passed muster at Oxbourne. The encounter proved a great success and not at all the ordeal by fire that Clare, and possibly Paul himself, had feared and expected. Her mother was enthusiastic, twittering attentively while he was there, gushing over the phone that evening and posing questions that were premature.

As they approached the south porch, the door creaked open and the Reverend Virgo emerged, the familiar bunch of keys jangling at her belt. Clare did the introductions.

"I'm just off to St Mary's, in Nestling," breathed the rector, as if sharing a secret known to few. "Valentine has some thoughts about maintenance of the churchyard. It's one of his days there."

"He's churchwarden at St Mary's too?"

"No, no. He goes to tend his wife's grave. I say 'wife'; it happened before they managed to…all rather tragic. It was well before my time. I never met her myself but my predecessor thought it prudent to brief me."

"I'm sorry. I had no idea," said Clare. "What was her name?"

"Let's see. It was…Rachel something. That's right. Rachel Pollard. She lived most of the time in London with her father Martin. He was due to move to Danby Hall with her – he was to have the family suite, as it now is – but he never did."

Thirty-three

Dido brought Clare a cup of coffee while she was waiting in reception for Paul to finish his call to New York. On the other side of the road figures wrestled in the window of Venetia Spalding Fine Art with a large bronze statue of a horse. It was a rusty orange-brown in the light of a nearby street lamp.

She had kept up the practice of leaving chambers at a civilised hour and often avoided taking work home. Tonight, they were joining Jessica and Duncan for a meal in Camberwell (his wife was apparently at a conference in Harrogate) before going on to some jazz in the basement of a disused warehouse. The weekend before, she had invited all of them round for supper at number twelve and outlined the story of the locket, the book finds and her encounter with the sickle man. It seemed the best way of putting matters to rest, even though some of them knew some of it already. Clare did not, she said, want to probe further into what had happened to whom, at least for the time being. That included Valentine, from whom she had had a brief note apologising for 'being a trifle reticent' that day but saying no more. She resolved to send him a card at Christmas.

If there were thoughts that the level-headedness of her account contrasted with her own actions in the affair, these were not voiced on the night. There was some discussion in the sitting room afterwards of what she had said about the identity of the man with the sickle but no one had any suggestions to make beyond urging her to remain vigilant, despite her insistence that the incident would not recur. Even Clare thought it best to keep her *Tyto alba* theories to herself. Paul and Jessica agreed on the phone next day that Clare was in need of a holiday.

A prolonged rapping on the front door the following week brought Clare scurrying from the garden. She had been gathering windfalls from next door's overhanging pear tree, a welcome break from the work she was supposed to be doing at home. A brief fish-eye view through the spy hole was enough to reassure her. She twisted the key and pulled the door open.

"Colin! What are you doing here?"

She gave her brother a hug and dragged him inside. She took him into the kitchen and sat him at the table.

"Just passing through," he said, removing shoulder bag and jacket and leaving them on the floor. "On the off-chance. I've got an audition later. In a church hall in Lambeth. I must work out where it is."

"More Shakespeare?" She had seen him in Paris as

the King of Navarre in Ken Westow's Enigma Theatre production of *Love's Labour's Lost*.

"I'm up for Hal: *Henry IV, Part One*. There's a lot of competition for the part, Ken says, so nothing's guaranteed."

"How's Bryony?"

"Closeted in the flat, trying to learn her lines. Not a big part but it's on the telly and it's a series so she should get herself noticed. It's something to do with recovering stolen art treasures. Talking of which, I hear you have an art treasure of your own. You kept quiet about him."

Clare flushed and grinned.

"His name's Paul and he runs a gallery. I knew him at college and met him again by chance."

"Well, the parents are most impressed. I've just spent a couple of days at Oxbourne and got the usual earful. It's hard work being feckless and not doing a proper job."

He bent down, opened his bag and retrieved a copy of the play.

"I was told to give you this," he said, removing the envelope that was slipped inside. "Mum said you might like to see it. She wants it back."

The envelope was addressed to Augustus Newton Esq at a house in Kensington. The writing was a little shaky but Clare recognised it at once. The sender's own address was in south-east London, one of a number noted in the exercise book in the filing cabinet upstairs. The letter was dated 18th March 1929.

Dear Augustus,

I was sorry to learn of the death of your father. It is a great sadness, although I know he had not been well of late. He was always kind to me and we shared a love of the classics. Many years ago we read the poems of Catullus in the park and had an ice cream afterwards. A small memory but a precious one.

You may have heard from Sarah that we chanced to meet at Victoria station. She has scarcely altered. There was time for a cup of tea in the refreshment room. She told me that you have a grand-daughter, Isobel, who is already at school. I am delighted. It seems strange, when I think back to our days at Great Danby, that you and I should both be grandparents, if a little belated in my case. Young Martin is walking already and shows a lively interest in the world around him. Perhaps we might arrange for him and Isobel to meet and get to know each other. Sarah said she is minded to give Isobel when she is older a locket she has put away, a locket in memory of Beatrice. Poor, dear Beatrice. There is not a day goes by that I do not think of her.

With warm wishes,

Yours ever,

Ruth Pollard

Epilogue

The first floor of The Golden Goose had been transformed. Not by the tinsel, fairy lights, glass balls strung above the bar. These were regular seasonal additions. It was the stage, built up and out for the occasion, the glittering backdrop, the expanded space for musicians at the side. Between stage and bar, chairs and tables were tightly packed, tea lights refreshed and waiting for the off. It was nearly time but people were continuing to arrive, squeezing to their places, waving and calling to those they knew.

Clare had been asked to hold the date well in advance. The invitation itself arrived in the post a week or two before the event, not long after she and Paul got back from the Seychelles. It had gilt lettering on a violet ground, similar to one of the smaller cards that had been slipped through her letter box in the summer.

"Very smart," said Paul, eyeing the invitation propped against a jug on the dresser she had recently acquired from Verily Vintage. ("It was a bargain. Honestly: half-price in their pre-Christmas sale.") He had been invited too. They sat near the front at a table shared with Jessica and Duncan, the bottle between them a rich garnet-red in the glow of a tea light.

Jessica had been pleased with the watercolour of Bawson's Clump, now hanging in her house in Camberwell. "It keeps changing," she said, "depending on the weather and the time of day. Every time I look I see something different." She suggested giving one of the pictures of the cottage to Norman Filbert, the man they had met in the tea room at Brockley House the day they went to the cottage itself. "It seems right. He knew the place and the artist too. And, of course, he gave *me* a peacock once: the Meissen one by Kändler. I've moved it to be near the picture."

Clare had decided to keep Nathan's other picture after all. It was above the fireplace in her bedroom, the green of the cottage door as fresh and as bright as the grass in the foreground. Whether Marigold had told Iris that some of her father's paintings had been found in a former junk shop Clare did not know and had not asked. Neither did she discover how they had ended up there in the first place.

She twisted and shifted her chair as best she could. She was not keen to be in the Parslows' line of sight, even now. She waved discreetly to Marigold, sitting on the other side of the room with Lucy Potter and Anthony Buffo, to whom Clare had eventually returned all but a handful of the books. He would take nothing for them. She gave Paul a nudge to acknowledge Marigold, whose paintings had sold, against expectations, in the Christmas show at Bainbridge and Murray. She flushed as she realised that the necklace Iris had given her was having a rare public outing. The locket and chain were stowed securely at number twelve.

A man in a black tee-shirt nipped on stage to make a final adjustment to the three microphones standing at the front. The band members sidled to their seats, feigning lack of interest in the proceedings, then struck up in unison at the tap of a baton. The house lights dimmed, the stage was bathed in radiant silver-white. A voice from nowhere, "Ladies and Gentlemen. It's been a while but they're back at last. Will you welcome, please, Iris, Evie and Joan: the Celebrated Sydenham Chanteuses."

They began with 'Chattanooga Choo Choo' and finished with 'Jingle Bells'. The applause was long and loud, the call for more insistent and fruitful. The sisters swaying, shimmering in peacock green satin, Iris looking years younger, thought Clare, and all with their father's eyes and high forehead.

After the show was over, Iris made her way towards them. Her progress was slow, waylaid by admirers and well-wishers and those reminiscing about the old days. Paul stood up to let her sit down.

She sank to the chair, tired but exhilarated, eyes shining.

"It feels like we've never been away," she said, reaching for the nearest glass of wine. "Maybe we should have got back together sooner, when we were younger and had more energy. Who knows how things might have developed. Makes you think, doesn't it? Perhaps there are four tenses: past, present, future – and what might have been. That one is harder to predict."

Also by Christopher Bowden

The Blue Book

Fear death by water. D.

The discovery of a cryptic note hidden inside a second-hand book sends thirty-something Hugh Mullion on an obsessive search for its previous owner. Hugh uncovers secrets that have lain hidden for sixty years and turn upside down his views of personal identity and the certainty of the past. Along the way, Hugh learns more about himself and what he really wants from his relationship with his partner, Kate – and about the puzzling disappearances of Anthony Buffo, in whose shop Hugh found the book that changed everything.

"…an intriguing and affecting story written with élan… the kind of book that readers love."

The Yellow Room

When Jessica Tate finds an old country house guide in a box after her grandmother's funeral she is drawn into a mystery that has remained unsolved for over half a century and is set to change her life forever. Intrigued by the house and the family that lived there, she is propelled into a world of disappearances and deceptions, eventually unlocking the secret of the Yellow Room itself.

As the shadows lift, a picture emerges of a landed family fighting to stem the decline in its fortunes in a post-war world in which Britain's own role is steadily declining.

"…a rare glimpse into our recent history, far too rarely plundered by modern novelists, and deftly done." *Andrew Marr*

"A novel as intriguing as the house at its heart. I loved it." *Julian Fellowes*

"…quintessentially English…an intriguing book, full of family mysteries and deception." *Oxford Times*

The Red House

Her face was thinner than it used to be, tauter somehow, almost gaunt, and the eyes seemed troubled. The hair, once long and flowing, was cut roughly short. Almost hacked, he thought. Yet it was surely her...

When Colin Mallory sees a sketch of a young actress he once knew on display in the local market, memories of their past together are brought back sharply to the surface. Alarmed by her distressed appearance, Colin is propelled on a search that draws him into the nightmare world of 'the group' and the sinister influence that threatens to control him too.

This is an engrossing story of artifice and hidden secrets, rich with theatrical detail and a cast of compelling characters.

"Very entertaining, cleverly constructed and expertly paced. I thoroughly enjoyed it." *Sir Derek Jacobi*